Tankh

Tankhem

Meditations on Tantrik and Egyptian magick and
the mysteries of Seth, the Great Dragon

by
Mogg Morgan

Published by
Mandrake of Oxford
PO Box 250
OXFORD
OX1 1AP (UK)

A CIP catalogue record for this book is available from the British Library and the US Library of Congress.

ISBN 1 869928 865

Contents

The god names and other common terms are given according to
the standard Greek convention, for example Isis, Osiris and Seth.

1 Prolegomena to Egyptian magick

At the beginning of the twentieth century mystics were fond of the notion that our human story could be arranged according to developmental aeons or great periods of time, usually blocks of approximately 2000 years, determined and ruled over by the succession of constellations in the Zodiac. Examples of this belief can be found in groups such as the Hermetic Order of the Golden Dawn, whose magick was, in essence, a revival of Egyptian modes. Egyptology and the Golden Dawn seemed to peak at the same historical moment.[1]

It has always interested me how, to paraphrase Umberto Eco, even a false history can change the world (see *Serendipity*). Ideas that were once the provenance of a tiny group of obscure mystics, have, in the intervening years been repackaged and taken seriously even by less gifted theologians and thinkers. To me this implies that the imaginal world peopled and explored by magicians can, and often does, give birth to ideas that can live in the 'real' or material world. In 1960, Georgio de Santillana, published a book called *Hamlet's Mill* that floated the hypothesis that changes in religious ideas could be provoked by changes in the heavens. Our understanding as a species could have been greatly expanded by knowledge of the phenomena of precession (more of that in a moment).[2] Many wish to extend this reasoning into the future, and maintain that the current changes in the 'star markers' may also be having some effect on the modern psyche - the so called birth of the age of Aquarius.

As we move forward in time mystics appear to be looking backwards. Some would say that the future is more real than the past. The past is the past, all its elements are gone or its threads, if they do persist, are shells, like decayed foundations, on which newer structures have, of necessity, been built.[3] Whereas the future is in formation, the elements that will make it are here now, like straw, ready to be blended with mud bricks to make new buildings. In a wonderful metaphor Wittgenstein wrote that reconstructing the past was as futile as trying 'to repair a torn spider's web with our fingers', it cannot be done.[4] The inference I draw from this is that reconstructing the past is essentially an act of magick.

Why would anyone at the end of the twentieth century be interested in the ideas of so long ago - we can argue about how long. Current philosophical thinking would probably maintain that the growth of 'do it yourself' religious movements is evidence of a strong irrational current within the modern world - an argument against the notion of intellectual progress and a counterpoint to the belief in progress based on scientific thinking (see John Grey, *Now History is Over*). This assumes of course that humanity's religious quest is not a rational endeavour, except where represented by state and orthodox religion. But I contend that occultism and magick is rational and that an interest in reviving ancient cults is part of the process any self-aware person goes through. They must, of necessity, make for themselves a history, a chain of causes and effects that have brought them to this moment. It may be that you can graft the work of professional historians into your own story. But nowadays there are so many contradictory accounts of the past, you must still make a choice, otherwise you are destined to vacillate between one account and another. The more you look at it, the more it sometimes appears that the writing of history is some form of game we play with ourselves. You must make your own synthesis, your own way through.

Some like to describe the activities of magicians as 'post-modern' in the sense of taking ideas and themes from an ancient, seemingly moribund past, and giving them a new content, making them work or become relevant for now. Some of us understand instinctively that there are certain preoccupations that were shared by the Ancient Egyptians and ourselves. It has taken the best part of the last century for the whole intellectual community to focus on the nature of consciousness. At first it seems that consciousness (and indeed unconsciousness) was the discovery of modern minds. But slowly the realization has dawned that these issues have been addressed long and hard in other cultures, often very ancient ones. Now the question is finally revealed as an interesting one, the search is on for data, perhaps any data, from our long past, that casts any light on the psyche and its progress. For example the Jungian psychoanalyst Charles Poncé wrote that the Egyptian creation of the otherworld beyond the horizon is parallel to the modern psychotherapeutic creation of the unconscious.[5]

If you are the kind of person who thinks this way, then your personal philosophy may demand that you seek the oldest ideas available. You may find yourself inexorably drawn, as many before have been, to the writings and artefacts of ancient Egypt. One way to understand how a complex thing is, is to look at how it begins. Santillana's hypothesis is that the origins of human consciousness lie in the contemplation of the shifting fortunes of the stars - or more especially in the unravelling of the mysteries of the precession of the equinoxes. Poncé took the less controversial line that contemplation of the revolutions of the northern constellations were what first gave us rationality, in the sense that the world then fulfilled the function of a clock.[6]

If you already have a fair understanding of the concept of precession - you might find the next few paragraphs fairly old hat. The earth is an irregular sphere that rotates on its own axis approximately every twenty-four hours. In addition to this diurnal motion, the earth is in orbit around the sun. However the axis of the earth is not exactly parallel to the axis of the sun. There are several small wobbles in the mechanism and given a long enough period of time, and consistent observation, the earthbound star watcher would notice small irregularities in the motion of the stars. Whether or not the ancients quite saw it this way is largely irrelevant, the effect is real and sooner or later, any long standing civilization will need, so the argument goes, to make adjustments to its calendar in order to take account of these irregularities. The most commonly recognised calendar problem for the ancient world was known as the precession of the equinoxes.

Elementary astrological lore refers to the apparent path of the sun visible from the earth, as the zodiac, astronomy knows this as the ecliptic. The zodiac, is a notional band of bright stars, grouped into constellations and given the names of mythical animals, hence its name, *Zodiac*, from same Greek root as our word *zoo*. Of course the Greeks weren't the first to observe and map these constellations, but they certainly put the science of star watching onto a more precise standing. The Greeks also popularised the familiar order of the zodiac beginning with Aries and ending with Aquarius. This order of the zodiac tells us that the year begins or 'opens' with Aries the Ram and closes with Aquarius, the water carrier. Its like one of those old fashioned wind up clocks, if you forget to wind it and it stops you can tell the time at which it was last wound by a simple process of deduction. The same principles can be applied to the universe that surrounds us and indeed, the zodiac.

Let us assume that the beginning of the year is going to be at the spring or vernal equinox. You could therefore reasonably expect the constellation of Aries the Ram, to be visible at some significant point in the night sky on or around that date, which if you don't know is 21st March. The significant point is called its heliacal rising, the constellation will rise just before dawn on the appropriate day. Just say you are what is known in the popular parlance as an Aries, one who was born with sun in Aries. You may be taken with the idea of getting up before dawn on your birthday in order to see the constellation Aries, the Ram, rising in the eastern horizon just before the sun comes up and with its light, obliterates sight of the stars altogether. However, if you do this you're in for a disappointment, as the constellation would *fail to arrive* on time. What you would actually see rising just before dawn on or about 21st March would not be the constellation Aries the Ram but a totally different constellation - Pisces!

In the intervening 2000 years or so since the 'clock' was first wound up, the spring equinox constellation has changed. Aries is in fact hours away from rising and even the constellation Pisces only just peeps over the horizon before dawn. To use the words of Jane B Sellers,[7] 'It is as if the whole wheel of the zodiac has been *dragged* back by almost thirty degree of arc.'[8] This dragging back is not something that has happened overnight but the accumulation of tiny variations in the orbit of the earth around the sun (1 degree every 72 years). These may be tiny variations, but over the course of several thousand years they add up to an observable change. This phenomena of the *dragging* back of the constellations is known as precession.[9]

This failure of the equinox star marker to *arrive* on time might be disappointing to the modern viewer but it is hardly earth-shattering. But try to imagine the effect this 'failure to arrive' might have had on our ancestors. Some say that the priesthood may have had to work very hard to explain this failure of the constellation or equinox marker to arrive and open the year. Bear in mind also that in ancient Egypt, these same constellations were considered to be gods, some of them quite high up in the celestial hierarchy. Living as we do now in well lit cities, we have perhaps lost a great deal of our former contact with the heavens, and therefore awe in respect of the great spectacle that is played out every night above us. Sometimes on a clear night on some darksome and lonely hillside, it is possible to recreate some of this ancient reverance for the sky.

Of course the constellations are an illusion, an act of magick, mental constructs or to use a less loaded term they are, abstract entities. In reality the distance between them could be colossal but their virtual magnitude makes them appear as a group. Constellations are humanity's earliest exercise in virtual reality or if you prefer abstraction.[10] It is interesting to speculate how much ancient peoples shared similar views of the heavens. Some of the constellations shown on Egyptian star maps cover vast tracts of space and are probably peculiar to them. Others, such as those found in the zodiac are recognised by people as widely diffuse as ancient Greece and South America. Constellations do seem to have an intersubjective quality. (See Vera J Gilbert)

You can tell from the order of the zodiac that it was invented at least 4000 years ago, when Aries really did mark the vernal equinox. An idea as complicated as the zodiac would seem to require a certain lead time to develop and most authorities seem to think that the earliest of this kind of zodiacal observation was completed during the age of Taurus (the zodiacal sign that follows or preceeds Aries). It is therefore reasonable to suppose that the primitive zodiac has been around for more than 4000 years.

But did the ancient Egyptians know these things? Most Egyptologists think not. From ancient Egypt, many early star maps have survived, either as papyri or painted and inscribed on the walls of tombs, temples and coffins. These texts clearly show that forms of gods, such as Isis, Osiris and Seth were associated with certain star groups. It is not too startling to think that the Ancient Egyptian gave god names to the constellations and planets they could identify, they gave god names to almost everything else with which they came into contact. Its still a moot point as to whether the Egyptians viewed these stars as anything more than a metaphor, a divine correspondence, a map but not the thing itself. (Surely this is implied by the fact that the constellation's name may be grammatically determined by one god but be named after another).

You might wonder what difference it would make to them. But consider how difficult it would be to plan in the absence of a reliable calendar. Knowing when the year starts, when winter will come, when possible dangers of flooding of planted crops might arise, etc etc, all this can be important. What if you had planned a nice beach party for the local head piston-sprocket which is then washed out by the 'untimely' rise of the local river. Joking aside, it seems reasonable then to suppose that, in our past, the cycles of the stars may have taught us some important lessons, and that they may even have contributed towards the growth of what we call consciousness and the complexities we know as culture and civilization. The observation of the Northern stars would certainly be an aid to navigation and seems to have played an important role in the regulation of the lunar calendar, the earliest form of agricultural planning. Observation of the moon is an important prerequisite for the construction of tide calendars, and therefore an important aid to any seafaring community.

That the ancient Egyptians knew the secrets of precessions seems, as yet, unproved to me. But one phenomenon they did in fact observe with some precision, was the northern constellation they called Meskhetyu[11] and which in the modern era is known as Ursa Major or the Plough. And it seems a likely fact that this was a skill they did not invent but one that they learned from their predynastic and Neolithic ancestors. We all know this constellation, its the easy one, and therefore often ignored. If we find it easy, perhaps our ancestors did likewise. This constellation was known by the ancient Egyptians as one of the imperishable stars, a group of northern, circumpolar stars. There's an obvious spiritual thought - when I die, I go to the imperishable stars - they do not perish.

'Oh my mother Nuit
stretch yourself over me
so that I may come to lie in the imperishable stars
that are in you and I shall not die' -*Pyramid Texts*.

Of course not all ancient cultures are star gazers. People who live in deep forests (or brightly lit cities) have precious few opportunities for accurate star watching, due to the absence of a clear horizon. It would be a bold anthropologist who would speculate on the difference in consciousness and intellectual history that the absence or presence of an horizon might engender. But leaving that question aside for other minds, let us merely underline the fact that star-gazing needs a horizon, such as the sea or treeless landscapes. Perhaps we have stumbled on the beginning of one of the first major abstractions of our intellectual history - the concept of an horizon and of something that lies beyond.

As is well known, the great pyramids of Giza exhibit a remarkable degree of accuracy in their orientation to the meridian. I.E.S.Edwards, one of the acknowledged experts on the pyramids, says that this can only have been done with reference to the Pole star, although the exact method by which this was done can only be guessed at. We have to say guessed at, for although it is clear that the Meskhetyu - the Plough, was always used as a marker of the pole of heaven, the modern method would not have worked then due to precession.[12] An exact description of one method is only given in texts of a much later period, for instance from the Graeco-Roman temples of Dendera and Edfu. One of these texts describes a method to calculate the northern orientation by reference to the Great Bear constellation. It seems to be the case that many of the texts at Edfu contain information from a much earlier date, some of it even conjectured to be older than the pyramids. All of which serves to underline the fact that this knowledge was very old, even for the Egyptians and may well have been passed down from Archaic and Neolithic times. (see Edwards, *The Pyramids of Egypt*, p.256sq).

As if to underline this point, a group of archeologists recently published a remarkable discovery from Upper Egypt (Southern Egypt). About 11,000 years ago, the southern African monsoon migrated northwards and this normally arid region became very green and fertile. Archeologists have found the remains, near Nabta, of a late Neolithic settlement. Nabta is right on the border between modern Sudan (ancient Nubia) and southern or Upper Egypt. The archeologists seem to be implying that the archaic settlers of this region followed the monsoon *northwards* from Africa. For several thousand years a small agricultural community thrived here in what is nowadays barren desert.

This settlement of a few dozen houses, has a most remarkable feature, a small stone circle, very like those more well known in Europe. Does this imply that the circle builders of Europe

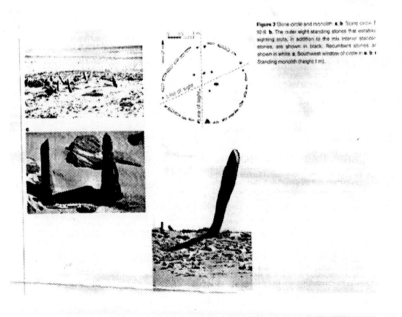

Figure 3 Stone circle and monolith. a, b. Stone circle 92-8. b. The outer eight standing stones that establish sighting axis, in addition to the two interior standing stones, are shown in black. Recumbent stones are shown in white. c. Southwest window of circle. d, e, f. Standing monolith (height 1 m).

originated in Africa - that's interesting food for thought? The circle and subsidiary ritual site (include a cow burial) exhibit strong Northern and Solar alignments. How could these ancient people have made a northern alignment? In the absence of a compass the only other known method is by observing the position of the Northern constellations. The ability to make such a calculation would have been very useful to these people in their navigation of the ocean of sand known as the Sahara desert. (See *Nature*, Letters, Vol 392/2nd April 1998). The authors speculate that these same people later moved down into the Nile Valley, their social organisation already well developed, thus laying the basis for the predynastic society of ancient Egypt. And indeed in dynastic Egypt the northern constellation[13] The Plough - Meskhetyu, is associated with the god Seth, whose people were said to come from Nubet or Southern Egypt, not too far from where the stone circle was found. [14]

Another candidate for a stellar event that might well have meant something to ancient people, is the seasonal absence of the constellation Orion. Arguably one of the most spectacular constellations in the night sky. The Ancient Egyptians seem to have associated the god Osiris with this constellation Orion calling it Sahu. Osiris is one of those unfortunate gods who manages to get himself killed. It is possible to see this as a reflection or gloss upon the 'behaviour' of the constellation itself. Orion is a southern constellation visible in the night sky for most of the year. In dynastic times Orion first began to 'disappear' from the sky at around the spring equinox, nowadays, because of precession this

would be around April or early May. It reappearance in the night
sky approximately 70 days later. This period of absence may be
approximately the length of time required by ancient Egyptian
ritualists to embalm a king's body - so by a stretch of the
imagination this annual rising and then decline and death does
seem to parallel the mythology of Osiris, the source of the ideology
of the dying and resurrecting god. I suppose I should touch upon
the fact there are a whole bunch of books that have a lot to say
about Orion and the pyramids etc. I don't think what I say cuts
across the ideas in many of these books because I am largely
sticking to, what to me, seems the more obvious parts of the
mythology, things that are perhaps, so obvious that they are missed
out in the theories advanced by these authors. For example, Jane
B Sellers passes over the idea of seasonal absence in one sentence,
and plumps instead for a more speculative theory based on
eclipses.[15]

Magical hermeneutics

It might seem to you that the approach I take to this material is a
mixture of mystical inspiration and book research. This kind of
approach is not without precedent as it is the normal methodology
of theology. Interestingly this approach is often given the technical
name Hermeneutics, which basically means to interpret. As I
understand this discipline, the interpretor enters into the very thing
he or she is attempting to explain, so in some sense the arguments
are circular and from a formal point of view not objective. It is
rather like the idea that one has to believe in order to know. I

suppose in the final analysis one judges this kind of thing on pragmatic grounds. So the interpretations, however generated, hold together and make sense of the material and do they yield predictions that are later corroborated by other lines of thought.

I was first led into all this by a circuitous route. I started as a believer and practitioner of magick. The variety of magick that influenced me was not mainstream, even in the terms of the pagan community. Perhaps because of my own background, I was drawn to the fringes of magical belief and I felt an affinity with the outsiders of mythology. Every mythology has its outsiders, in the Abrahamic tradition it is Shaitan, Satan, Iblis, the Devil or whatever.[16] Just as above I described the natural propensity of philosophy to draw the thinker back in time towards the genesis of an idea, so too in my quest for outsiders, I was drawn to their Egyptian manifestations.

An interest in supposed 'evil' or dark archetypes is not such an unusual thing in the modern world although it can put one in bad company. It seems to be that a great deal of the thrust of psychoanalysis is about confronting and integrating forces that at one time in our history would have been thought best ignored or even suppressed. One of the many analytical tools used by magicians is the tarot deck. I was very struck by some of the differences between cards designed before the popularization of Freud's theories and those created afterwards. This difference is most noticeable in a card such as the Devil. In the pre-Freudian decks, the Devil represents sexual instinct but this is always seen as a negative force that enslaves humanity and obstructs further spiritual progress. In decks after Freud, such as Crowley's *Book of Thoth*, the devil still represents rampant sexuality, but now seen as a potentially liberating force, the instincts are no longer seen as negative forces in our psyche, but as very positive indeed. These new tarot decks seem to be telling us that we must look again at what is only seen by the majority as a wholly negative and obstructing force, perhaps things are not as they seem.

So I looked again at the history of the Devil and this naturally enough brought me to the source of many of our ideas about evil, as they were first written down, many thousands of years ago in dynastic Egypt.[17] Anyone for whom this is all familiar territory may be expecting me to now introduce the strange god form known as Seth, who according to most standard accounts of Egyptian religion is often said to be the ancient personification of evil. Assume for a moment that ancient cultures actually had a concept of 'evil'. This is an assumption, as it is widely believed that the concept of *absolute* evil is a peculiarity of the Abrahamic tradition. Ancient cultures are said, so the argument goes, to personify some kind of negative force but this is always a relative thing, what is bad for some may often be good for others.

The oldest personification of 'evil' is in fact a serpent 'deity' called Apophis or Apep. As far as I can tell there was never any ancient cult of Apophis - Apophis is not the demonised god of another rival cult. The most common account of Apophis is as a vast cosmic serpent that is so large and chaotic that it threatens the journey of the very sun itself and can only be derided by the collective actions of all the gods, including Seth. Perhaps the origins of Apophis lie in some destructive natural phenomena, things falling apart and going wrong for no particular reason. For example an earthquake or perhaps some cosmic catastrophe such as a meteorite hitting the earth. The greatest evil of which the Egyptians, and perhaps we can conceive, is the end of all this, as it will all end in umpteen million years time when our own sun finally does succumb to Apep and burn out. Evil then is that which threatens our human existence with extinction. That's assuming that we haven't managed, by our own efforts, to bring either our existence and maybe that of other lifeforms, to an untimely end.

Egyptian religion is quite sophisticated although this was not the opinion of the Egyptologists of the early part of this century. You have to bear in mind that these ideas have only been available to us for a relatively short time. Before the translation of hieroglyphs in the last century, what was known was at second hand from the accounts of ancient Greek philosophers and historians and these, we were told, needed to be treated with a big pinch of salt. Even so, the ideas of ancient Egypt were, to use the words of the advertising copywriter, full of eastern promise. What emerged was, for many, so perverse, that the study of these things as important religious ideas was virtually abandoned. From the standpoint of the modern mind, the texts do not seem to be very systematic. We may know the literal meaning of what was said but the meta-language used is, to many, a closed book they would prefer to leave closed.

Nowhere is this more evident than in the ancient Egyptian's attitude to the 'evil' god Seth. Once again we encounter something unique, a god who starts good and becomes bad. (By the way that is another first for the Egyptian theologians). What I call theology is really nothing more than the efforts of the Egyptian priests to construct a family history of the gods that were most important to them. Even a cursory look at the material shows that the Egyptians were polytheistic and saw themselves as completely surrounded, almost submerged in divine forces. They recognised hundreds of gods and goddesses, although there was obviously some kind of hierarchy, if only because some of these forces have vast amounts written about them, whilst others must of necessity remain obscure for the simple fact that the only thing we know of them is their names mentioned in maybe one or two places. Modern theologians are steadily coming round to the idea, commonplace in orientalism, that polytheism is a rational approach to humanity's religious experience.[18] Our psyche is seldom influenced by one pure force, there are conflicting and rival gods at work. At the very least we might expect male and female forces to be there. If some mystics do encounter the One, it can only be in the world beyond gender and as it exists in the abstract realm of pure spirit - but this is not the world we most of us move in or have the clearest understanding.

The Egyptians cut through the proliferation of gods by imposing on it a family structure they called the 'company of heaven' and we call an Ennead[19] or Ogdoad. These families of gods form a magical or symbolic system which is the nearest they got to our concept of theology. The most famous of these families are those of Heliopolis (the On of the Pyramid Texts), Memphis (Thinis) and Hermopolis (Egyptian Hmnw or Town-of-the-Eight).[20] These are the systems of which records have survived, although it is fairly safe to assume that the priests of other urban centres also had their favoured views of the holy family.

The Temple of Seth

For personal magical reasons I was led to investigate a totally different Ennead, that of Abydos, the cult centre of Osiris in the ancient world. Although my reasons for avoiding the more well trodden theologies may seem capricious to some, I soon learnt that the Abydos system is acknowledged as an important if neglected theological view. The idea of analysing a belief system from a single 'node' of a whole network of beliefs is well founded in European intellectual historiography.[21] I am an amateur Egyptologist and all amateurs are best advised to confine their studies to a very narrow field, and Abydos seemed at the time to be a fairly manageable area for my magical and historical research.

Even so I do take certain liberties with the system, the justification for which the reader will have to wait until a later chapter. The Abydos theology or company of gods, is set in stone in the design of one of the most unusual temples of ancient Egypt, the temple of Seti I or as he sometimes called - Sethos. Sethos was named after the Egyptian god Seth, which speaks volumes for how they viewed the god at that period in their history, approximately 1350BC. The temple design is unique, as it has shrines of equal status for each of the seven gods of the company. Temple design normally consists of a shrine for the major deity accompanied by the immediate members of his or her family, whom outside of the temple might play relatively minor roles in other cult centre's pantheons. Thus the famous temple of Amon at Luxor has subsidiary shrines for his son Khonsu and his consort the vulture goddess Mut.

At Abydos the seven shrines stand side by side of equal size and status and this is very suggestive of a theology. In the central line of the temple is the holy of holies of Amon, the mysterious creator god. To each side of the shrine of Amon lie respectively the shrines of Rahorakhti a form of Horus, Ptah, an earth god, and the deified form of King Seti. For reasons that will maybe become clear, I think we can also associate King Seti with the god Seth, ie treat this shrine as a shrine of Seth. (This is the kind of big assumption that only a magician could make). To the right of the Amon shrine are arrayed shrines for Osiris, Horus and Isis. This is a greatly simplified view.

The reason for this gerrymandering of the temple lie in the fact that, apart from some fragmentary remains, there are no surviving shrines of Seth. Unlike the chaotic Apophis, there definitely was an ancient cult of Seth but as Egyptian society developed, the cult of Seth fell into terminal decline and his holy places were largely erased. In order to learn something about this cult I had to look at the many traces of the cult as it survived in other places, paradoxically some of the most useful information came by looking at the temple of his supposed victim, Osiris, whose cult centre was at Abydos.

The first thing that struck me about Seth was his form. Here's a picture taken from a Middle Kingdom wand (c.1800BC), carved from hippopotamus ivory, and exhibited in the National Museum of Scotland, Edinburgh. The male hippopotamus was another of the zoomorphic forms of Seth.

You see an image of a canid of some kind maybe a dog. If you look closely you see features that are not seen on any living creature; the nose is strange and the ears are, from a zoological perspective, unnatural. The Egyptians were quite capable of making very fine naturalistic depictions of animals. In fact they exhibit a great affection for the animals that surrounded them and some of their observations are very naturalistic indeed. Here's an example, which although not the best I could find does have the advantage of coming from the same artefact as the Seth image and is therefore a good point of comparison:

The ancient Egyptian reverence for the natural world, coming as it does at such an early stage in our history, is, in itself, very

revealing of the Egyptian psyche. I think it is fairly safe to assume that within the conventions of Egyptian art, the non-naturalistic depiction of the god Seth is deliberate and not the function of mere artistic naivety.

The zoomorphic image of Seth, often shows a forked tail and sometimes this image morphs into what looks like an arrow sticking into the dog's behind. There has been a fair amount of discussion about this beast in Egyptological publications. There is a controversy as to whether this image is intended to be a representation of an actual beast or is purely mythological. The jury is still out on that and my own opinion is that the image is not intended to be taken as a piece of zoology. This is a purely mythological beast, and, significantly so I believe, it is drawn in such a way that the viewer cannot really mistake it for a real animal. So this immediately divides it from virtually all other images of the gods - where the combination of animal and human, where is does occur, as in for example in this unusual winged Nuit, taken from the coffin of Seti I, all the elements are naturalistic (The wings are wrapped around her body to form a dress). Seth has to be seen as, strictly speaking, a monstrous entity in his own class. There are other unmistakably mythological beasts, such as the griffin, but these also are often associated with the cult of Seth.

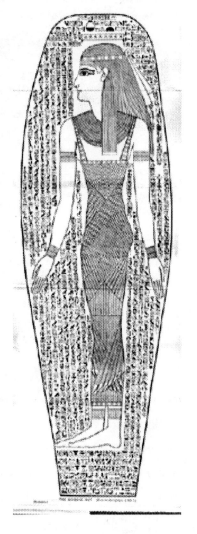

Now images of Seth are very old even in Egyptian terms. Along with our hawk-headed friend Horus they are amongst some of the oldest religious icons to have survived from prehistoric times.[22]

I am interested in teratology, the study of monsters. Sometimes the monstrous is a more efficient way of expressing a mysterious religious doctrine. For example, much of the iconography of Hinduism is quite monstrous and this is said to be an expression of the doctrine of 'inappropriate symbolism' - ie the image is so obviously not the reality that the onlooker is forced to look for inner meaning.[23] In the analysis of Hindu iconography, there are two important ways in which deities get their form, some such as Krisna-Visnu, seem to represent human qualities such as the father or husband writ large as deities. Another path to the divine is seen in for example the cult of Shiva, who seems to represent a human psychological trait, recognised and transformed into a divine entity (which comes first is a moot point). Whereas animal deities could be said to represent animal qualities, such as strength or sensitivity, made into divinites, monstrous dieties may represent human qualities, perhaps unpleasant ones, personified. It is this later hypothesis that I favour for the analysis of Seth, who may represent certain human qualities writ large or recognised in a divine entity. Whichever way you look at it, the image of Seth represents an extremly old exercise in abstraction and human psychological reification.

What might these qualities be? At some point in our development as human beings a tension arose between the physical requirements of humans as successful omnivores and a sense of empathy with the animals and sometimes plants, which we must kill in order to survive. Taken to its logical extreme, this tension led to the growth of vegetarianism in the Indian sub-continent around about the time of the Buddha in the sixth century BC. Other cultures chose to live with the tension and accept that in the final analysis everything, including ourselves is food or is part of the food chain or chain of being. The ancient Egyptians method of dealing with the tension was to personify many of the natural, if repugnant, aspects of human life into the form of monstrous deity called Seth. Seen this way, Seth represents only a relative evil. Seth is still part of the family of gods, although one with a clearly ambiguous nature.

Egyptian civilization was the fruit of the Nile, which was able to produce a massive agricultural surplus. It is undoubtedly this capacity of Egypt to feed the then known world that accounted for the greatly prized nature of the colony to both the Greek and Roman empires - it was literally their food bowl. But this great plenitude was in turn founded on an annual and in many instances disastrous flood of the Nile. This may be a clear instance of where human well being was founded on largescale 'evil' and destruction for others, notably the creatures killed by the flood, as indeed the land, personified as Osiris, was drowned and flooded by 'cosmic' forces each year.

Any functional society relies on the presence within it of individuals who are capable of actually doing the unthinkable, whether that be slaughtering an animal for food or indeed ridding society of what it considers to be its sociopaths by judicial execution or warfare. These are all qualities attached to the cult of Seth. His capacity for rational and irrational violence was recognised by the early Egyptians as a vital part of a functioning society. Society in this context means a politico-religious state whose basic building blocks were the extended human family group.

Other important but ambiguous functions of society were also personified in Seth. Apart from Seth's capacity for violence Seth also represents society's libido in all its forms. That Seth should be the personification of raw sexuality shows that these people recognised both the necessity and, occasionally, negative aspects of sex. Seth was seen as both a lover of women *and* of men. Whereas other deities, such as Isis, may well be brought into play to represent fertility and fecundity, Seth is hardly about reproductive sex at all but almost solely about the raw power of sexual desire itself - or if you like, non-reproductive and recreational sex, both of which were important aspects of ancient Egyptian society. It is in this area of the power of sexuality that Egyptians show streams of thought closest to our own modern sensibilities. After a long hiatus, the second half of the twentieth century witnessed the rediscovery of the ability to control our fertility and enjoy and use sexuality for its own sake. This is a remarkable parallelism. It is in the above contexts that I will explore further the spirituality of Seth and his family in subsequent chapters.

Magical thought experiments

If the ancient Egyptian god Seth does represent aspects of human psychology writ large and deified he also represents, as perhaps all the gods do, a human construction. He may well be, to use a magical term, a thought form. This may well be at odds with some reader's expectation of how they see the genesis of the gods, it may seem quite an anti-religious view. Maybe this is so, perhaps the gods, or at least some of them, are entities to which we, as human beings, give birth. This does not prevent these thought structures taking on a life of their own, taking on some independent existence, althought their original conception, if such it can be called, is in many ways an act of unconscious magick. That such structures should be capable of independence from their creators is not such a strange thought in the East, where no less a concept than our sense of the Self, is seen as a construct. As my old mentor once commented to me, the human sense of self is like a very tighted bound knot, whose loose ends have been hidden where they are nearly impossible to unpick. In Buddhism for instance, the knot of ideas to which we give the name the Self, can, under certain circumstances, be unravelled.

Modern magicians mostly agree that magick has no dogma, there is no one view of what the activity involves. It seems clear that magick is a part of, perhaps the origin of all religions. Even so scholars of ancient magick such as Hans Dieta Betz have advanced the thesis that magick can be seen as a unified religious view in its own right.

> *We should make it clear that this syncretism is more than a hodge-podge of heterogeneous items. In effect, it is a **new religion altogether**, (my emphasis) displaying unified religious attitudes and beliefs. As an example, one may mention the enormously important role of the gods and goddesses of the underworld. The role of these underworld deities is not new to Egyptian religion or, to some extent, to ancient Greek religion; but it is characteristic of the Hellenistic syncretism of the Greek magical papyri that the netherworld and its deities had become one of its most important concerns. The goddess Hekate, identical with Persephone, Selene, Artemis and the old Babylonian goddess Ereschigal, is one of the deities most often invoked in the papyri. Through the egyptianizing influence of Osiris, Isis and their company, other gods like Hermes, Aphrodite, and even the Jewish god IAO, have in many respects become underworld deities. In fact, human life seems to consist of nothing but negotiations in the antechambers of death*

and the world of the dead. The underworld deities, the demons and spirits of the dead, are constantly and unscrupulously invoked and exploited as the most important means for achieving the goals of human life on earth: the acquisition of love, wealth, health, fame, knowledge of the future, control over other persons, and so forth. In other words, there is a consensus that the best way to success and worldly pleasures is by using the underworld, death, and the forces of death. [24]

I think modern magicians would agree with a great deal of that although they may vary as to their opinion on the exact nature of the underworld. Some, would ascribe real ontological existence to its gods and goddesses. It is undoubtedly true that many magicians I have talked to experience a direct communion with entities that they perceive as existing independently of their own thoughts. Although I have no doubts that some magicians experience the numinous in this way, it has also to be admitted that there is a lot of pressure on the magician to *claim* their experience is so. I think this is what Tanya Luhrmann was getting up when she used the term 'interpretive drift' - magical peer pressure if you like. [25]

Others experience the presence of the divine in a more emotional way. As Poncé comments, if one adheres to a doctrine of correspondences between the gods and parts of your own body, a common enough magical view, then the activities of the gods will be experienced as emotions. [26] I have to confess that I share a great deal of this view, some of my most potent, even destructive, encounters with divine forces has been through my emotional life. It is almost as if I am taking on the persona of a particular god or goddess, this seems to draw certain people into my orbit and this leads to unexpected life experiences and emotional involvements, some of which seem parallel to the mythology of the god invoked. I have worked for many years with the god Seth. An important aspect of Seth's mythology seems to involve quite challenging situations. Seth, like Shaitan in the *Old Testament Book of Job*, is a tester. And I certainly feel that whenever I take up again the priestly duties of the cult of Seth, I am in for a testing time!

The notion of the underworld emerges first into religious discourse in the writings of the ancient Egyptians. It is the world beyond the horizon, and this we have already commented, is strangely similar to the modern concept of the unconscious. The idea that magick works with the unconscious mind, the world of the psyche, is another common enough view of modern magicians and is closest to my own. It only seems at odds with a more religious approach if the unconscious is viewed as a less effective world than the world of matter. Magicians soon learn that there are powerful links between this world beyond the horizon and the mundane world in which they exist. Some sorcerers, beginning with Aleister Crowley, Austin Osman Spare and culminating with the modern day Chaos magicians, have proved to their own satisfaction, that the unconscious is more effective at achieving certain things than the world of physical cause and effect.

I now approach the whole of magick as a thought experiment. Perhaps all experiments have a subjective element, but as much as any experiment can be objective, magicians believe that they are also able to be so. Part of the training of any magician involves the assumption of a belief system. It is said that the content of the adopted belief system is largely irrelevant although there are obvious favourites. Mostly the magician adopts as a belief system the material of the magical tradition itself - which in this particular corner of the universe is the Hermetic tradition, an identifiable magical tradition, whose roots lie in ancient Egypt. Although the magician adopts the system on trust, a suspension of disbelief if you like, he or she hopes that after a period of total immersion in that system it will, as it it were, go live. If this fails to happen, the magician will either drop the whole enterprise (not uncommon), try another system, or continue anyway but for other reasons. In the sociology of religion it is commonplace to make a distinction between the virtuoso practitioners, those for whom peak magical experiences seem fairly frequent and the more ordinary spiritual practitioners, for whom, being part of a movement has its own personal rewards. These rewards might be involvement in interesting historical research. Snoo Wilson in his novel *I Crowley* talks, tongue in cheek, about the *lesser* magick of authorship, which is another product of magick with which many of us are content to fill our lives. Some find joy in supporting other virtuoso practitioners whose results are tangible and interesting. And yet others hope that spiritual development might eventually come in the course of time. Magick, if you like, becomes a way of life.

A lack of ability to make progress in the greater, more 'gnostic' aspects of magick is no obstacle to success in the lesser forms of magick, including results magick or the casting of spells and sometimes curses. The fact is that many of the techniques of 'results' magick, such as construction of talismans, seem to work regardless of the operator's degree of mystical attainment. This kind of activity is fairly common amongst modern magicians, as indeed it was in ancient times. Some might object that the ability to work results magick is predicated upon mystical advancement. For example, the magical acts of tantrik magicians of South Asia is said to be dependent on the execution of quite complicated daily magical devotions. I like that idea but think that most magicians would admit that a great deal of results magick seems to work *regardless* of the inner state of the operator. Also it has to be said that magicians, certainly in the past, will often fulfil a magical task on someone else's behalf, even if they have doubts about their own ability to really make it work!

The above considerations apply to the magical community now and I think is quite likely that they applied to the magical communities of the past. Some of these may account for the fact that magical communities of the past were not always popular. Under the rule of Roman Emperor Augustus, magicians and witches had become enough of a nuisance to the state that Augustus passed laws that began a long period of book burning and general repression. This was long before the rise of Christianity, so one wonder's what they had done to bring this on themselves. And one also cannot but reflect on the decline in status of the workers of miracles, from the time of Egypt's golden age, when magick and religion were synonymous. The reaction was so strong that even the Egyptian language, once used by ancient magicians, became a dead language and those buildings which bore its inscriptions sank below the sands of the desert, only to re-emerge after several millennia of dreamy sleep.

I wrote earlier about the occult doctrine of the ages of humanity, as ruled over by the stars. An occultist might suppose that the dawning of the age of Pisces, heralded a change in people's attitude to magick. The poet W.B.Yeats, for instance, 'discovered' or 'invented' a whole development of this idea. He divided history up into spirals or gyres, the beginning of one embedded in the end of the other. Magick declines when it becomes attenuated. 2000 years ago it was at the end of something, it was at the ultimate point of its development - it would have to collapse, overcome by its own inconsistencies. According to this theory, any religion has a natural lifespan or cycle, and will in the long run become corrupt and devoid of its original sense of meaning. 2000 years on, the time is right for the beginning of a new cycle, the age of Aquarius may also be the time of the rebirth of magick although in some radical new form.

I've deliberately strayed into some awkward issues in connection with magick, I feel happy to try and describe magick, warts and all. Other magical practitioners prefer to skate over this or pretend it only happens elsewhere. This can make a great deal of magical writing little more than propaganda. These negative issues aside, I still believe that magick is a rational and intellectually respectable pursuit. I try to live with its tensions and take an experimental approach that avoids some of the worst pitfalls. Afterall, there are aspects of any intellectual tradition that may be unpalatable but it is only the fanatic who would reject the whole enterprise because of some resolving questions of value. Lets not forget that modern science has some powerful critics, worried by some of its methods, eg: vivisection or its application such as military conquest.

An approach to magick is by the construction of magical thought experiments. I use this term to mean that one makes certain assumptions and then immerses oneself into the magical tradition by learning about it history and techniques, seeing if you can make them work. I now believe I was led to the study of Egyptian magick. A linked series of coincidences suggested the study of the temple of Seti I at Abydos as the area on which I should focus. I had spent several years before that picking away at the edges but my guides indicated that the time was right to go deeper. There is in fact an inner pattern to this that may be familiar to others. Magicians start work using an elemental (indeed elementary system); over time their magical symbolism switches to the use of 'planetary' forces, and given enough time, their focus will turn even more outward (or is it inward?) to the realm of the fixed stars, felt by some to be the most subtle form of cosmic energy that has any influence upon us. No-one reading this account would believe that I was being at all objective and I have to agree. But I was happy in my own mind that I retained sufficient healthy scepticism and distance from the material. Apart from hitting the books, my main method of inner work consisted of forming mental reconstructions of the temple. I have been quite pleased with the results. Of course the use of thought experiments and visualisation has nothing intrinsically occult about it. Anyone approaching a complex system of ideas would be well advised to form some sort of mental model that they can view in their mind's eye from several perspectives.

They can walk through it if you like, seeing how it functions in various imaginary situations. Even a surgeon attempting to resolve some difficult piece of anatomy has recourse to these kinds of visioning skills.

On purely pragmatic grounds I count this ongoing thought experiment as a success. I feel I am viably reconstructing a version of the ancient Egyptian magical religion. The model or system I am developing increases my knowledge and enables me to make inferences and predictions. These factors show the model is pragmatically sound. The description of the main details of the system will have to wait until a later chapter. The major early discovery was in the symbolic significance of the cardinal direction North in mythology, indeed in my own psyche. Consideration of the implication of northern alignments and northern symbolism has emerged as a 'secret' key, not only to Egyptian magick but often becomes the connecting link across cultures. I couldn't say whether this is really a magical secret or something that is fairly obvious to anyone who looks at the magical tradition itself. After I'd reached this conclusion I had a nice confirmation from another magician. Stephen Flowers, in his excellent book says that 'One of the least discussed, yet most powerful aspects of astral mythology and star-magick is that which surrounds the Polar region of the night sky - dominated by the Bears and Draco - with the Pole Star in their midst.'[27] When I read that I knew I was onto the right track. Although I do not follow all of Stephen Flowers conclusions, I felt that my magick had given me a genuine piece of knowledge that, for whatever reason, I did not have before. And this knowledge could be used to work more magick, sometimes with startling results.

The experiment continues. The essence of this kind of magick is orientation. All magick worth its salt, seems, sooner or later to lead the operator to a consideration of themselves and their relationship to the cosmos. Whether this be by the use of astrology or the acquaintance with the other patterns of the stars as they flow around us. Magick attempts to place the individual at the centre of his or her universe. It is not so much that the position of the constellations and planets at birth determines the temperament and constitution of the subject. It seems more likely that the person already has these things hidden within their psyche. They are sensitive and react to cosmic forces, even if they are unaware of the full range of possibilities. A useful concept here comes from the Tantrik tradition, itself a survival of ancient Egyptian magick. In Tantrism a great deal of emphasis is placed on deconditioning. Tantrism starts with a concept of the person, fully formed and possessed of temperament and constitution, given by birth and upbringing. Many elements of this conditioning are felt by Tantriks to be inimicable to the spiritual progress of that individual. Bad habits and social mores have crept into the psyche unnoticed and the Tantrik seeks to examine these traits one by one, stripping away what is unnecessary or arbitrary. What remains, so the theory goes, it the essence, and this essence is spiritually free and perfected. One of the techniques of Tantrism is indeed the study of astrology and cosmology, both of which are seen as powerful aids to deconditioning. This is at odds with the erroneous view that magick is deterministic, it is not.

Through this kind of stellar magick, the operator gains insight and is able to align his or her psyche to the cosmic forces around them or at least take account of possible sub-conscious forces in their acts. Magick aims I suppose, at the perfection of the self by the study of the self. Magick also aims at the perfection of wisdom, which can only come when all of the complicated chains of causes and effects is cognised either in full or part. Some might say that this is impossible, it is as futile a task as reconstructing Wittgenstein's famous spider's web. Well that is the issue that divides the sceptic from the mystic. The mystical mind claims to be able to cognise such a complex model. How to express this might be another matter, but it is the opinion of the present author that such insights are possible. I've set out in general terms the method to approach this. It merely remains to describe in greater detail the particular thought experiments I use. It is up to you whether you choose to follow this path or construct your own version based on hints given by the magicians of the past. That's the fun, I hope you enjoy the journey.

Notes

1   An interest in things Egyptian has been around a long time, despite the fact that the Egyptian language was then, a dead language, it had not been spoken for several thousand years and all attempts at interpretation of the texts was largely inspired guesswork. Any real facts about Egyptian religion and magick were known only at second hand from the

writings of ancient Greek and Roman 'historians' such as Plutarch's *Isis and Osiris*. These are still the source of most people's view of Egyptian magick. But Egyptomania really did get a boost from the Napoleonic wars, when Champollion, an archeologist attached to Napoleon's army, made the first successful translation of *Hieroglyphics* based on the trilingual texts of the so-called Rosetta stone (now in the British Museum).

2   Giorgio de Santillana & Hertha von Derchend, *Hamlet's Will - an essay investigating the origins of human knowledge and its transmission through myth* (Godine 1969)

3   It seems that the stars have always provided a reference point to the past, according to modern astronomy, we are currently observing them as they were in the past. Genetics is another axample of the past effecting the future, ancient peoples were also aware of the mixture of their ancestor's blood in the current generation, although they did not call it genetics.

4   Wittgenstein, *Philosophical Investigations*, 106

5   Charles Poncé, *The Archetype of the Unconscious and the Transfiguration of Therapy - Reflections on Jungian Pschology* (North Atlantic Books, 1990).

6   Op cit

7   Jane B Sellers, *The Death of the Gods in Ancient Egypt* (Penguin). A fascinating, informative but in my opinion flawed - flawed because of its obsessive quest to make all ancient mythology reflective of the phenomena of solar eclipses.

8   The apparent 'dragging' back of the stars occurs as a rate of 50 seconds per year, so that over 72 years, the drag will equal one degree of arc. (interestingly the Babylonians, who were precocious star-watchers, used a calendar system based on a five day week, 72 weeks a year). Assuming 360 degrees in a complete circle, means that it takes 72 x 360 for the stars to return to point their starting points - 72 x 360 = 25,920 or the number of years in a so-called great year.

9   And by the way, if you fancy checking this out for yourself, do it by actual observation not by looking it up in an ephemeris. Most modern ephemerides use the zodiac as a virtual band and take no notice of the actual position of the zodiac. Modern astrology is not really based on the influence of the constellations, these are merely convenient bench marks. Astrology actually plots the relationship between birthtimes and rising planets and to do this all one needs is a fairly simple schema that can ignore precession altogether. Only in certain more esoteric forms of western and eastern astrology is the actual position of the planet vis a vis the constellations taken into account, the so-called sidereal systems of astrology. Astronomers and sidereal astrologers must either make their own observations or make a conversion between the data given in a standard ephemeris and the actual position of the stars, roughly speaking by adding five days and subtracting one sign.

10   I will continue to point out some of these abstractions, if only for the reason that modern scholars are fond of stating

that the ancient Egyptians were supposedly a practical people not given to abstract thought - plainly this is not true - the ancient Egyptians gave us several major abstractions, including those, which according to Kant are virtually the ground of our being - space and time.

11   See astrological ceiling in secret tomb of Senmut (vizier of Hapshepsut) see Clagett p. 116

12   To find the pole star in the modern age, follow a line between the two outer stars X and Y and the first star you come to will be the pole star, in fact Polaris in Ursa Minor (the little Bear). This would not have worked 4000 years ago.

13   W Hartner, 'The Earliest History of the Constellations in the Near East' and the motif of the Lion-Bull combat.' JNES 24 (1965), pp. 1-16, 16 plates.

14   It occurred to me that it might be interesting to see whether similar northern alignments could be found in the more wellknown stone circles of Europe. This is perhaps a feature passed over in various published analyses of neolithic ritual. But even a cursory look at the collection of stone circle surveys published by Thom and Burl, shows that a northern alignment is perhaps one of the clearest features of stone circles, even more so than other solar features. See *Megalithic Rings*, A&A.S. Thom and A. Burl (Bar British Series 81 1980). Here's the plan of the Rollright stones (Hrolla-landriht 'Rolla's land') in Oxfordshire (SP 296309 51° 58' 1° 34'). The stones have been disturbed quite a lot, so it certainly not the best example, but it is my local stone circle.

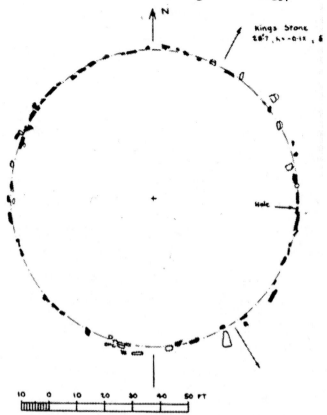

Kings Stone

15   Sellers, op cit, p. 42 'I am convinced that if the death of Osiris is to be found in the movements of the constellation Orion, it lies in something more than Orion's seasonal absence resulting from the regular movements of the sky.'

16   See *Myth of the Magus* below.

17   The western concept of the 'devil' may be inspired by the ancient Egyptian Seth but I doubt if the Egyptians of the Middle or Old Kingdom would recognise the two concepts,

it has been warped so completely.

18   See Danielou, *Shiva and Dionysus*

19   Ennead from Greek meaning nine, ogdoad - eight.

20   The Heliopolitan ennead consists of Amon-ra etc; Memphis
        heads of with Ptah, whose cult centre was in Memphis,
        Hermopolis has a more conceptual system of paired
        complementary gods, amun - amunet etc.

21   See for instance the work of Michel Foucault, who reveals
        many interesting dynamics in European society from
        research into un-selfconscious records such as legal reports
        and scientific praxis.

22   This seems to make images of Seth far older than images of
        Osiris, his future victim, although some try to argue on the
        basis 'that absence of evidence is not evidence of absence'
        ie that the cult of Osiris was so all pervasive and self-evident
        that it was never discussed - I have problems with that line
        of argument.

23   See Partha Mitter, *Much Maligned Monsters* etc. This might be
        in constrast to the Greeks who seem to have been in love
        with surface and produced very few monstrous images of
        their gods.

24   Hans Dieter Betz, *The Greek Magical Papyri in Translation*
        (University of Chicago Press 1986) Vol 1, P. xlvi-xlvii

25   Tanya Luhrmann, *Persuasions of the Witch's Craft* (Blackwell)

26   Ponce *op cit*

27   Stephen Edred Flowers, *Hermetic Magick - the postmodern
        magical papyris of Abaris* (Weiser 1995) p.200

2 Setanism

'Satanism is a minor aspect of A[leister] C[rowley]'s work, and
to label it, him or Thelema as Satanic misses the point in favor
of pejorative sensationalism. Yes, there is a relationship between
Thelema and Satanism There is no mention of Satan in Liber
AL. Not even Seth, in the pseudo-Egyptian idiom. If Crowley
was a Satanist, or if Thelema was Satanism, one would think
that he would have spent a lot more ink on the subject than he
did. (from internet)

Thus is sometimes claimed to be the orthodox Thelemic position,
if, sadly, such a thing can be said to exist. In what follows I intend
to undermine the above argument. I guess that all of us at some
time or another have felt the attraction or glamour of Satanism -
I am going to argue that the best place to look for this current is
within the Thelemic community. I'm not sure if this is contentious

- most people associate the Egyptian god Horus with Thelema - and Horus is not particularly satanic. But I have a confession to make - I'm not particularly into Horus and have never really understood why Crowley was.

As far as the popular understanding of Satanism goes, as for example reflected in the tabloid press, we can, with a clear conscience say no, Thelema is not satanic. Thelemites are certainly not satanic in the accepted meaning of the term. The real story is simply too complicated to share with the general press. But aside from this, it has to be said that Satanism is a reasonable interpretation of the Thelemic system and one that does stand up to intelligent scrutiny. It may be that Satanism, or perhaps we should adopt the older spelling Setanism, is a reasonable and intellectually viable position for the *modern* magi to adopt.

I suppose when people think of satanism they automatically think of the overtly satanic magical orders such as the Church of Satan and its offshoot the Temple of Seth. There are also some more obscure groupings such as The Order of the Nine Angles and The Brotherhood of Seth. These are interesting groupings, but as far as I can see, a lot of their magick is pretty much derivative from the Thelemic/Crowley based orders, although given a more satanic spin. It's a while since I've looked at the written material from these satanic orders, so best check this out for yourself. A few years back a whole panel of speakers from the Temple of Seth spoke at the Symposium of Thelemic Magick, hosted by Oxford Golden Dawn Occult Society. The result was a bit unsatisfactory. We heard a great deal about hierarchies and exalted grades but very little about the actual mythology of Satan or Seth. It strikes me that given the nature of the Seth archetype, magical orders with a very strict grade structure, would not be the way forward.

Anton LaVey founded the Church of Satan in 1966. It seems to be a mixture of show business and magick - no problem with that. Anton LaVey was an interesting magician, with a bit of a wild reputation. Anton LaVey who played the devil in the movie *Rosemary's Baby* died of pulmonary edema in San Francisco on October 29th 1997 at the age 67.[1]

Bit of a synchronicity here - as I was writing this I received a series of phonecalls from a couple of Satanists working their way through LaVey's *Satanic Bible*. They asked me a few questions which made it fairly clear that they hadn't looked at any of Crowley's material. This surprised me and I said so - as far as I am concerned, Crowley ought to be the first stopping point for any would be Satanist. My informants told me that LaVey warns against using Crowley because he disliked his well known drug addiction. This seemed an odd taboo to find amongst Satanists! So that's it - followers of a *drug crazed* guru Aleister Crowley are in danger of giving Satanism a bad name! The more cynical might say that LaVey was worried that would be recruits might find a richer vein in Crowley's writings. Very few occult writers are completely original and it might be that some of LaVey's work does rely on Crowley, The Golden Dawn and other predecessors. Most of us can live with that. From what I was told - LaVey could do with absorbing some of the technical instructions given in for example *Liber ABA - Magick*. Apparently LaVey makes no mention of the correct way to vibrate god names - on which, drug addict or no, Crowley has some important things to say.

It is said that before he developed his Satanic stage show LaVey's act included a bit lion-taming and he regularly put his head in the beast's mouth. The Church of Satan has a mixed reputation amongst other occultists. LaVey is said to be quite right wing in his social and political leanings. There was a recent underground documentary about the murderer Charles Manson, made by The Werewolf Order - another offshoot of the Church of Satan - headed up by Nicolas Shrek and Anton's daughter Zeena LaVey. In their film they say that LaVey hated the hippy generation of the sixties and ritually cursed it. This all happened a few days before the Manson murders of Sharron Tate *et al*. Historians often say that the Manson murders signaled the end of the sixties - Manson, who by his own admission, also hated the hippy philosophy but was nevertheless seen as the iconic hippy thing and a warning of the dark excesses to which the sixties philosophy of 'Do what thou wilt' might lead.

Despite this Anton LaVey's magnum opus *The Satanic Bible* is a perennial best seller and the basis of much Satanic ritual. As far as I can remember - the *Satanic Bible* works with lots of god forms from the medieval grimoire tradition. For instance Belial - a Hebrew name meaning 'worthless' or 'destruction', widely used in the middle ages as a synonym for Satan, or the Devil. I suppose the problem with this kind of material is two fold. Firstly its power hinges around the unconscious power of the Christian or Abrahamic demonology. A lot of us are trying to get away from defining our magick in terms of Christian concepts. Although it has to be said that they do retain a lot of residual power and they can be a useful way of deconditioning. Maybe it's as Ray Sherwin once said - every magician should perform a black mass as least once in his or her lives. This sort of Satanism is a good way of getting going but what do you do when the concept of the Christian devil really is empty of any emotional charge? A lot of magicians are constantly on the look out of peak experiences. Psychological fear is a very easy way of getting a cheap hit - especially if you are the kind of person who gets a kick out of the hammer house of horror type magick. This can all be a useful process but if you're not careful you can find yourself on a ever increasing spiral of extremes. To get the same hit you must define ever more and more 'frightening' rituals - and if that fails - you may in desperation try something anti-social or illegal. Going to jail for your magick may seem a cool idea - but I suspect that things might seem different when you're actually staring at four white walls of your prison cell. A lot of the glamour of this kind of magick is based on scaring yourself or your friends to death. And some magicians are happy to confine themselves to that. They just want to be seen as powerful magicians, someone to be feared or dreaded. Some people find that a useful survival technique.

A second problem I have with this material of for example *The Satanic Bible* is that it is a corrupt version of the ancient originals. The demonologists who wrote it had very little interest in getting the mythology spot on. Thus for example one reads of invocation of Astoreth - drawn as a male demon - when modern research has shown there was no such ancient diety and that Astoreth is a confusion with Astarte, the ancient Mesopotamian goddess - who is not particularly demonic - except in the sex starved ravings of the Christian monks. To be fair, modern Satanists are aware of these facts but choose to work on, or reclaim these mental constructs. The gaps in the satanic pantheon have been filled by some using a text called the *Necronomicon*. The *Necronomicon* is a very good spoof put together by fans of the paranoid horror writer H P Lovecraft. I've no problem with magicos making up magical texts - but I don't really share Lovecraft's horrors concerning the 'nameless ones'. For it seems to me that the ideas in his books key into a vision of the universe where inhuman and dark forces are waiting for a crack to appear in our psychic armor, so that they can return from their long exile in hyper-reality. I don't really buy that, although it was put to me by Jan Fries that some of the better versions of the *Necronomicon* unashamedly plunder the Sumerian magical tradition. It may be bad to take a known mystical tradition of the ancients and purvey it as part of the satanic mythos - but at least it gets people looking at ancient magick. Hopefully they will ditch their *Necronomicons* and start using the real McCoy.

One of the problems about identifying yourself as a Satanist is that it puts you in bad company. Isolated occultists tend to hear more negative things about magick than positive. The newcomer to magick may be looking for something to oppose their early religious conditioning. As many of us are brought up in the Abrahamic tradition (Islam, Christianity or Judaism) - we have it drummed into us that if you're not for example a Christian then you are one of Satan's own. In the absence of accurate information, the strong willed type may say, well fuck it, if to be against all this Abraham shit, I have to be a Satanist, OK, I'm a Satanist. Occasionally some adopt all the media clichés of Satanism and devil worship and even end up the wrong side of the law.

It is interesting how this popular image of the Satanist has changed over the last few decades. When I first got interested in magick, the dominant 'authority' was someone called Dennis Wheatley - difficult to believe that now! (Ask yourself - if it is viable to spin a whole magical system out of H P Lovecraft's horror fiction then why not Dennis Wheatley? His lurid novels with titles like *The Devil Rides Out* and *To the Devil a Daughter* once gripped the popular imagination. Dennis Wheatley, who was/is politically at least, a very right wing writer, thought that the archetypal Satanist would have to be a *communist*. In fact the satanic figures in his books were quite glamorous types, rich, famous but also members of a secret fifth column. Satan's plan for Britain was communist revolution. It was a fact that there were a group of patrician Oxbridge types such as Blunt, Berges and Maclean, who had been recruited by the KGB to spy for the Russians. I used to read Wheatley's books under the bed-clothes at night and at the time I was rather communistically inclined. Like many I found the satanic characters in his books much more attractive than the Christian protagonists. It's funny how since then, the 'satanic' torch has been taken up by much more right wing groups. I think I'm correct in saying that some of the leading lights in say The Temple of Set, are also supporters of the right wing, perhaps fascist National Front?

It has given Satanism a bad name. The fascist but otherwise eminent prehistorian H Winkler, speculated that the 'Shemsu Hor', the mythological 'Followers of Horus' , and not the Confederates of Seth, were the true antecedents of the Aryan brotherhood.

I have much more time for the Surrealist version of Satanism - it's my prejudice if you like. They seem to have adopted Satanism as a corrective to the Catholic church. See for example Salvador Dali's painting *The Profanation of the Host* painted in 1929. The Surrealists were encouraged to insult nuns and priests whenever they met them in the street. Perhaps this gave Crowley the idea to recommend that his followers greet any priests with the phrase 'apo panto kaikadaimos' - get away from me all evil. Although according to *Remembering Aleister Crowley*, Kenneth Grant's memoir of the master, Crowley was horribly embarrassed when Kenneth Grant took him at his word and did the deed. Deconditioning is one thing, but we live in a multicultural multifaith society and there are real dangers to stirring up sectarian hatreds. My own motto is live and let live - and it may surprise you to learn that the ancient followers of the Egyptian God Seth, from whom we get a great deal of the Satanic mythos, were also quite tolerant of other people's spiritual choices.

The Myth of the Magus

More often the occultist meets others or discovers Crowley and discovers there are lots of different ways of being a magician. Satanism is a powerful glamour that has projected many of us into the magical life - most end up doing the right thing for what were initially wrong or poorly understood reasons. The easiest way into this is to take a look at a thing called the 'Myth of the Magus'. I assume that all who read this have an ambition to be a magus, to be one of the magi. Well it may surprise some of you to learn that there is actually an established myth of the magus, and it is a very old myth indeed. Crowley was a magus. The term magi, from which we get the term magick etc, is of obscure origin. It is a very ancient word. Some think that the magi are some kind of 'caste' or ethnic group that have existed throughout human history. In modern psychoanalytic language, perhaps the magus is a personality type.

In ancient society, the magus always had a dual nature - not thought of as wholly evil or good. For a good example of the magus personality at work before the time of Jesus Christ, see Euripides *The Bacchae*[2], in which the central character Dionysus uses black magick for possibly 'good' ends and where 'a religion of indescribable beauty, rapture, holiness and joy prevailed over an uninspiring official cult by inhuman, indeed devilish means.'[3]

This ambiguity was largely tolerated until about 2000 years ago when there was a bit of a sea-change[4] in attitude. This of course coincides with the growth of Christian cult to world religion but the process of 'demonization' of the magus had probably begun a little before that in the reign of Augustus. Crowley was way ahead of his time in recognizing JC as a fellow member of the 'caste' of magi. This claim has been tested in several important books. I think Crowley liked to compare himself with Jesus Christ! Perhaps one of JC's most powerful pieces of magick was the destruction of the magus archetype itself. We owe it to JC for more or less creating the concept of the wholly 'wicked magus' or impostor with whom the Christian magi did battle. But really the magus is some sort of ancient hero figure. The life of a magus is said to have ten distinct elements, present either in part or full:

1. The Magus must have a mysterious or difficult origin
2. There may be omens at his or her birth
3. Perils menace his or her infancy
4. There must be an initiation
5. Wandering in distinct and strange lands in search of secret wisdom
6. At some point in the life of the magus there may be a magical contest of some kind
7. This is often followed by a trial or persecution
8. A last confession of some kind
9. A violent or mysterious death
10. A physical or intellectual resurrection.

It is possible to read this pattern in the life of most modern magi, including Aleister Crowley. If this pattern holds true then it is clear that the myth of the magus is rooted in ancient ritual drama.[4] The myth of the magus stems from some of the oldest dramatic texts to have survived from antiquity. One version is found in the *Canaanite Poem of Baal*. Perhaps that is too obscure - a more relevant version of the magus drama goes by the name the *Ramesseum Drama*. The Ramesseum drama was a seven act mystery play performed over seven days at different locations beginning at Abydos. It was timed to coincide with the subsidence of the flood and the moment the river became again navigable. This very ancient ritual drama tells the story of the royal/holy family of Egypt and the conflict of Seth and Horus.

The first generation is Amon-ra - the mysterious origin of the gods. His mysteries are those of masturbation. By a primarily act of masturbation Amon created the second generation, the wind and the air, Shu and Tefnut. After that he created the sky and the earth - Nuit and Geb. Their mysteries are those of sexuality and perhaps incest. These are obscure and sometime difficult to grasp. But from them issue a third generation or tier of celestial government - their children - Isis, Osiris, Horus (or Anubis); Nepthys and Seth. The mysteries of this third generation are basically the kind of things that go on in families - happy families and dysfunctional families. As all of us have some experience, good or bad, of family life, the holy family of Egypt has an immediate psychic resonance. One important thread within the story of the holy family is the famous or notorious conflict of Seth and Horus. This conflict of Seth and Horus - took place in the law courts, but also on a physical/violent level and also through magical battles. This drama was played out over several places and times, forming something very like the 'wheel of the year' rituals we all know and love.[6] It is this conflict that formed the myth of the magus. And it is the myth of the magi that Crowley lived, and that all of the magi lived out in their own lives, either consciously or unconsciously. It is an archetypal pattern of the magical life. It might be that there are two kinds of magi, those that identify with the Horus type and those of the Seth type.

A word on mythology

This mythology is perhaps the basic mythos of the Thelemic current. In order to use a mythology you do not have to believe in the physical or ontological existence of the gods themselves. To borrow a concept from chaos magick - it's a paradigm; a mental pattern that we can upload into our heads and then conduct an extended thought experiment. This generates interesting results.

In the drama of the holy family, all the players are important. Seth was born last and this causes problems. He is, if you like, the black sheep of the family - and as we know it is often the black sheep that ends up on the sacrificial altar. What is wrong with Seth from the Egyptian point of view? He wants his own way. This is also the supposed failing of all the magi during the last 2000 years. The magi want their own way - and their 'patron' Satan also wants his own way - see Milton *Paradise Lost* - 'Better to rule in Hell than serve in Heaven'. For this reason Thelemites have more in common with the character of Seth than they do with the character of Horus. The more you get to know about this ancient archetype, the more I began to wonder, why do Thelemites talk so much about Horus when the really interesting character is Seth?

The Horus aspect of the Thelemic cult has been under attack for several years now. One sacred text, *The Book of the Law*, has lots of typical Horus blood and guts and avenging angel stuff - fairly characteristic of the actual mythology of Horus. I view this as prophecy. *Liber Al* was published before all the carnage of the two greats wars - in some sense it was prophesying. But has the prophecy now been fulfilled? Many have thought it would be impossible to live for the next 2000 years under the kind of regime favoured by our hawk headed friend. Yes he is about in the world and needs to be given all due honour. But sanity requires that the reign of Horus can only be a short thing, the new age must be ruled over by a more egalitarian god form such perhaps as the goddess of truth and justice Maat. But Maat is only a minor deity in Egyptian mythology. All the gods in the primary holy family have had 'Maat' at some time or another.

It seems to me that the divine forces of the new age - cannot be put down to one god form - be that Osiris, Isis or Maat. Horus cannot rule the new aeon alone. It seems more likely that two forces, perhaps Seth and Horus, rule the new aeon psyche. Or perhaps it is time for all the Gods of the Pantheon - the god Ogdoas to 'rule' again? I want to come back to this later but for now will just say that this view is the Setian view. The philosophy of Seth is egalitarian and inclusive, whereas I think a totally Horus centered psyche would be very narrow. But I wanted to talk a little about the Setian or myth of the magus as it manifested in the life of Aleister Crowley - In essence I'm saying that Crowley lived his life as a magus in a way very like the ancient mythological life of Seth. Crowley was manifesting a pattern that is perhaps rooted in the collective unconscious. He was one of the latest in a long line of the magi - starting with Seth, but including Pythagoras, Simon Magus, John Dee, Cagliostro etc. We can also add some of the more cult figures like Mozart, Oscar Wilde and in our own times Elvis or David Bowie. (This correlation between the Myth of the Magus and characters like Aleister Crowley is explored elsewhere in a paper entitled 'Aleister Crowley and the Enchantment of the Wicked Magician'.)

The tracks of Setanism in Thelemic magick

I first got into this idea from reading Kenneth Grant's books especially *Aleister Crowley & The Hidden God*. I no longer completely agree with Grant's view but, credit where credit is due, it got me thinking on these lines. About ten years ago, I was engaged in a series of workings with the Egyptian deity Thoth or Greek Hermes. Thoth is another important part of the Thelemic mythos - Crowley called his tarot deck the *Book of Thoth*. And there was indeed a *Book of Thoth* known of in antiquity - although this was a book of magical spells and not, as far as we know, a divination system. However it may be that the original *Book of Thoth* contained special pictures and images. The story of the original book of Thoth is told in the legend of an Egyptian know as Setna or Satne. Technically, most magicians regard Thoth as the Egyptian god of magick and as a threshold guardian. He is the intermediary between the world of the gods and the world of people. Threshold guardians are invoked in order to open doorways and communicate with higher forces in the pyramid of creation. I soon discovered that in some accounts, Thoth is said to be the son of Seth. The son of any particular god is bound to have affinities with that god. Thoth, the ibis headed god, looks something like the traditional image of Seth. Thoth looks like Seth with his strange square ears removed. In ancient Egyptian material, pictures of Thoth were often substituted for pictures of Seth, which came to be viewed as unlucky (An example is reproduced in Katon Shual's *Sexual Magick*). The ancient Egyptians would have known that whenever a picture of Thoth appeared they might well understand that Seth is the actual force present.

In my magical work with Thoth I asked how I could learn more about his father Seth. The answer eventually came that I should look at the life and temple of the Egyptian pharaoh Seti I. It seemed a promising lead and I went to the Griffiths Egyptology library to study the plans of Seti's monuments. But to be honest I was disappointed - there seemed to be nothing there of very much relevance to the Setian mythos. It seemed to be a blind alley. Although Seth must have had cult centres in the past, history had dealt very hard with them, and followers of other cults came to demonize and neglect his cult and to obliterate his monuments. I abandoned this as a bad job, and didn't really look at it again until fairly recently.

For me one of the really useful techniques in modern magick is the use of the astral temple. This is a mental image or fantasy temple that the adept uses as an imaginary theatre for the play of his or her own will. I was teaching some foundation courses in magick and wanted to find a model for an astral temple that would use all of the ancient Egyptian gods and goddesses. I remembered the Temple of Seti I and took another look. This time the secrets began to reveal themselves. It would take too long to go into all that

here - but what I wanted to say that, what I know or believe to be
the essence of the real philosophy of the Setian, and indeed what
Satanism is, stems from my astral wanderings in this temple. The
temple is a real place and like any temple no part of its design is
accidental. It is a record in stone and paint of the Egyptian mythos.
It also fits quite well with the Thelemic mythos and tells lots of
interesting things about the ancient Seth cult - if you have the eye
to see it.

OK, consider the *Book of the Law, Liber Al vel Legis* one of the
holy books of Thelema. This book describes three sacred temples
or sanctuaries, side by side: one to Nuit, one to Hadit and the third
to Ra Hoor Khuit - ie Ra Horrakhty or 'Horus of the Horizon'. No
mention, as far as I can remember of Seth. I suppose it could be
argued that the presiding deity of the second book - Hadit - has
some affinities with Seth. But this is not altogether clear - *Liber Al*
chapter two starts:

> *'Nu! the hiding of Hadit. Come! all ye, and learn the secret that hath not
> yet been revealed. I, Hadit, am the complement of Nu, my bride.' (vs 1-2).*

The godname 'Hadit' is, as far as I know, based on what we
might call a scribal error. Crowley misheard the curator's translation
of 'Behadit' (Horus as the winged sun) as Hadit. It is easily done
if you're not too familiar with the conventions of Arabic
pronounciation. But once in the world the word has taken on a life
of its own, as a kind of post modern addition to the ancient
Egyptian pantheon. Hadit has much in common with Geb, a kind
of Egyptian Earth Deity and the consort of Nuit. The remainder

Setanism 63
<

of the chapter in *Liber Al* has lots of Horus symbolism, rather than Setian. My work with the Temple of Seti I, taught me that Seth, if he does appear, appears in a subtle or hidden form. The most obvious candidate for Seth is the discarnate entity that communicates the whole show. Maybe Aiwass, Crowley's HGA is Seti I. The objection might be that Aiwass says - AL I,7:

'Behold! it is revealed by Aiwass the minister of Hoor-paar-kraat.'

But even Crowley was unclear about the true identity of his own Holy Guardian Angel. This is very significant - most magicians I know, if they have made the contact at all, can usually quote chapter and verse about the nature of their HGA. Its a grey area and it seems to me that there is no real contradiction between the 'minister of Hoor-paar-kraat' still being a Setian. Crowley thought that Aiwass was Satan. He wrote in a footnote to *Liber ABA Magick* etc:

'The Beast 666 has preferred to let names stand as they are, and to proclaim simple that Aiwaz - the solar-phallic-hermetic 'Lucifer' is his Holy Guardian Angel and 'The Devil', Satan or Hadit of our particular unit of the starry universe. This serpent Satan, is not the enemy of Man, but He who made Gods of our race, knowing Good and Evil. He bade 'Know Thy Self' and taught initiation. He is 'The Devil' of the Book of Thoth. His emblem is Baphomet, the androgyne who is the hieroglyph of arcane perfection.' (p. 277 HB edition)

The Semitic deity Shaitan and the Egyptian Seth, are clearly spelt differently, although some clever linguist may well make a clear connection between them. But even without that, all the regular scholars seem to agree that struggle between the Old Testament deity Jahweh and the dragon, variously known as Shaitan or Samael, is yet another version of the ancient Egyptian fight between Seth and Horus where Satan is Seth.

Liber Samech

Assuming that Seth = Aiwass and that he is the secret communicator of the Thelemic mythos - how do we go about remaking this contact? Aiwass was Crowley's Holy Guardian Angel. The knowledge and conversation with one's Holy Guardian Angel was, and is one of the important magical tasks of any magican especially in the Thelemic tradition. Crowley wrote an elaborate ritual for one of his students to facilitate this contact. This all happened at Crowley's experimental community in Sicily. The student in question was Frank Bennett. Crowley prepared him by talking one on one about the nature of the unconscious - something must have clicked and Bennett fell into a gnostic trance. To consolidate this magical breakthrough Crowley penned a ritual that he called *Liber Samech*. Although this ritual was really designed with one person in mind, it has come to be seem as a model for all such rituals, especially by Thelemites. Bill Heidrick of the Caliphate OTO, in a private communication, told me that Crowley may have added the 'satanic' elements of *Liber Samech* just to wind Bennett up and that they may even have been inspired by the murals at the Abbey (those were a continuation of his Greenwich Village NY 'Dead Souls' style).

I'm not so convinced. The name of the ritual is significant - Samech - is the fifteenth letter of the magical Hebrew alphabet. It is the first letter of a word of power thought so powerful that it was best not to write it out in full - it is a code if you like. S - Samech is thought by most to stand for the Hebrew spiritual entity Samael - the blind one. This is the name used by the Hebrews as the major name of Shaitan during the Christian era. Blindness does have a link with the story of Seth and Horus - in one of their battles, Seth blinds Horus. Later in the saga the confederates of Seth are beheaded and being headless, although still alive, obviously has some deeper symbolic import but blindness is also a possible connotation. Thus when the ancient Egyptians opened one of the sacred shrines they said the following short spell:

'I remove the finger of Seth from the eye of Horus'

As they said it, they broke the seal of the shrine and slipped the iron bolt. Ancient Egypt was a bronze age culture but they did have small quantities of meteoric iron which was thought sacred to Seth.

But the Thelemic ritual *Liber Samech* has more direct connection with Seth. *Liber Samech* is based around a very ancient spell found amongst the *Greek Magical Papyri,* and which was circulated amongst members of the Hermetic Order of the Golden Dawn. It was known then as the Preliminary Invocation of the Goetia. Goetia are howling storm spirits. An ancient Jew who made a living painting hieroglyphs wrote the ritual. The first line reads 'Thee I invoke the Headless One'. The headless demon is one of the ancient names of Seth. (see Griffiths *Conflict of Horus and Seth*[6]) I don't think Crowley was aware of this. This is good - it shows that Crowley was being subconsciously led to the material. I don't think any modern commentators are aware of the direct connection between *Liber Samech* and Seth. It is not mentioned in the new HB edition of magick. Even Kenneth Grant, although he discusses this ritual in detail, seems to have missed that connection. *Liber Samech* is an invocation of Seth. This ancient invocation is in fact an exorcism rite that calls upon Seth to deliver x from the daimon which *restrains him* - or stops him doing his or her will.

'I am the headless daimon with sight in my feet; I am the mighty one [who possesses] the immortal fire; I am the truth who hates the fact that unjust deeds are done in the world; I am the one who makes the lightning flash and the thunder roll; I am the one whose sweat is the heavy rain which falls upon the earth that it might be inseminated; I am the one whose mouth burns completely; I am the one who begets and destroys; I am the Favor of the Aeon; my name is a heart encircled by a serpent; come forth and follow'

Seth is said to be 'powerful of foreleg'. All of the above attributes share a thoroughly Setian character. Before the ritual the magus prepares a special talisman marked with six names of power. The magus holds this over his or her forehead, and recites them at this point in the rite. Whilst doing this the magus faces north, the place of Seth. So that's the point - one of the most important rituals in the Thelemic cannon is in fact an invocation of Seth! He is called to control those demons that stop the operator from doing his or her own will. This clearing out of the psyche helps open a space for the HGA and the True will to manifest.

* * *

Aleister Crowley, a Magus of the new age, worked, perhaps unconsciously, with an underworld deity that wanted to be reintegrated into the modern world. Crowley knew that in the ancient pagan world there was no concept of absolute evil - god-forms such as Seth or Satan had a double nature. As Blavatsky wrote, what is good for some is bad for others. For example it does not make sense to call a volcano evil or the annual flood that drowned the vegetation of the Nile valley? Perhaps the eastern terms Yin and Yang are more appropriate aids to understanding. Yin and Yang are most often compared to the shadows on the mountain - they move according to the time of day, year, seasons etc. They are not fixed, what is yin one day, is yang the next. For Crowley - Shaitan/Seth was something like that. I have tried to argue that Setanism is a legitimate interpretation of the Thelemic current. But that these are ideas that need to be handled with care and discretion. I also believe that the source of a great deal of satanic magick can be found in the life of Crowley. Crowley's life provides us with an archetype in more ways than one. Crowley's life is the classic life of the magus, from strange beginnings to obscure end - his ghost rising from the dead years after his death to become a growing force in the spiritual wisdom of the new age.

Notes

1.   SAN FRANCISCO (AP) — Anton LaVey, who founded the Church of Satan in 1966 and played the devil in the movie "Rosemary's Baby," has died at the age of 67.Relatives said LaVey died of pulmonary edema on Oct. 29 at St. Mary's Hospital. 'Mysteriously, the death certificate states that LaVey died on   Halloween morning October 31,' said family spokesman Lee Houskeeper. LaVey was cremated on Tuesday after a Satanic funeral at Woodlawn Memorial Chapel in Colma.Security concerns led his daughter, Church of Satan High Priestess Karla LaVey, to demand 'absolute secrecy from all who knew of LaVey's death and Satanic funeral,' Houskeeper said. LaVey had a varied career before founding his church. He had been a circus lion tamer, an organist, photographer and psychic investigator.He first gained notoriety in 1967 when he performed his first Satanic wedding. He went on to write a Satanic Bible and four other books. He also acted as a consultant on several movies. His final book, *Satan Speaks*, was released in the spring of 1998. There are over a million copies of his books and each has been   translated into nearly every major language, according to Houskeeper. LaVey, dubbed 'The Black Pope' by some, leaves his daughter and longtime companion Blanche Barton and a 4-year-old son, Xerxes LaVey.

2   Euripides, *The Bacchae*, ed. Dodds, (OUP 1944) p.144

3   Butler, E.M. *The Myth of the Magus,* (CUP) p. 46

4   'Sea-change', term coined by Shakespeare in *The Tempest* - the transmogrification occurs at the bottom of the sea.

5   See Gaster, Theodor H., *Thespis - ritual, myth and drama in the ancient near east* (Anchor/Doubleday 1961). The Canaanite texts were discovered in 1930-33 at Ras esh-Shamra, site of the ancient city of Ugarit on the north coast of Syria. Gaster says they are written in a proto-Hebrew dialect. (p. 85)

6   It is now largely accepted that origins of the wheel of the year does not lie in Celtic religious ideas, but where then does it originate? Is it a modern creation, as some maintain or is it, as perhaps Margaret Murray implies, a 'survival' of elements of this myth cycle. See her article 'The Cult of Drowned' etc. I suppose we should add the caveat that Murray only took up the study of European folklore and witchcraft during the First World War when the Egyptology libraries were closed. For this reason she is sometimes considered as a bit of an amateur in this field although she was president of the folklore society between 1953 and 1955. In recent years the defects of her work on European history of witchcraft have emerged, although it would be wrong to completely discount all her conclusions. See her biography *My First Hundred Years*, published in the year of her death by William Kimber 1963.

7   See Griffith *Contending of Seth and Horus, Liverpool, 1960.*

3 Tankhem

Egyptian Magick and Tantra
(Hindu background)

I want to draw your attention to the connections between left hand path tantrism, alchemy and Egyptian magick. Many occultists have long suspected that tantrism and Egyptian magick are intimately connected. I think I first encountered this idea in the works of Kenneth Grant and it is one of the few that can sustain inspection. Perhaps the ideas survived in India following the loss of ancient magical knowledge, brought about by the rise of Christianity to the status of a state religion under the Roman despot Constantine.

In the third edition of my book *Sexual Magick*, I started to explore this theme in a chapter entitled, *The Erotic Landscape*. In tantrism spirit of place is keenly sensed. Tantriks call their sacred sites *Pitha*, which distinguishes them from orthodox Hindus who use the totally different term - *tirtha*. The tantrik pithas always designate a shrine of the primal goddess. For example in a very old tantrik text of my own (Nath) tradition, it is a place of pilgrimage as well as somewhere to sit and meditate. Pitha, which means 'seat' is also a piece of tantrik *twilight* language, and is a euphemism for the sexual organ.

These same ancient texts tell us that there are four important Pithas or pilgrimage sites. Sometimes a few others are added, making the total up to seven; sometimes one hundred and eight are mentioned, an especially auspicious number in this tradition; and sometimes they are said to be countless.

The origin of these pilgrimage sites is the matter of legend, and the details of this legend make it clear we are dealing with an eternal or archetypal myth; one that recurs in several other cultures. This may be called *the* tantrik myth. This is not just another tantrik myth; it is in some ways the core myth that explains a great many tantrik practices. I shall set out the story as it survived in Hindu and other texts. You've probably guessed that I am convinced that the myth is Egyptian in origin. And I am not alone in this view.

The first part of the myth

The myth revolves around the story of Sati, she who gives her name to the distasteful practice of widow burning in India. This is a social rather than a religious practice and the myth does not give clear sanction for such a thing. Sati was a goddess not a mortal woman and she chose her fate, whilst many widows are compelled to follow the goddess's 'example'.

[Sati] is the consort of Shiva and a personification of the goddess. Shiva and Sati have retired to their mountain paradise. Meanwhile Sati's father Daksha (whose name means 'ritual skill') plans a great sacrifice, to which he invites all divine beings with the exception of Shiva and his wife. Daksa plans this insult to Shiva because he does not approve of his alliance with his daughter for whom he may harbour incestuous desires. Incest, is also a strong driving undercurrent of the Egyptian version of this myth.

The insult [proves] too much for Sati who promptly kills herself. In some versions she flings herself onto the sacrificial fire, thus giving her name to the subsequent practice of widow self-sacrifice. When Shiva arrives on the scene he kills Daksa and destroys the feast, engendering many new human diseases.

I have argued elsewhere that it is possible to see the advent of several new diseases (Tuberculosis, Diabetes etc) in about the sixth century BC, as an historical reality brought about by the change from nomadic pastoral livelihood to ancient city life.

This part of the myth is very old, the oldest version traceable to the ancient *Rig Veda* and it may well be older. In medieval India, at the time when tantrism was at its height, this myth was again embellished. Shiva was too late to save Sati but he discovers the remains of her body. He picks her up and sobbing with grief, carries her about the universe. Eventually the god Vishnu is called upon to end this potentially disruptive situation. He follows Shiva, gradually slicing up the body of Sati. The four most magically potent pieces of her body fall to the ground and give rise to the four most sacred places or pithas of tantrism. These are her genitals, nipples and tongue.

In my opinion the most authentic version of this myth has Sati dismembered into either fourteen or twenty eight pieces. These are lunar numbers. In Indian calendar studies, the month is lunar and can be divided into twenty eight solar days. The month has two halves, a bright and a dark fortnight. The lunar calendar in India is very ancient and like astrology is derived from Babylonia. There is also a less wellknown zodiac of lunar days (tithis), which for reasons too complicated to go into here, are 1/32 in number and are also related to the Tantrik body magick of the kalas. In the ancient world these calendars were referred to either as 'by the god's reckoning' or 'by man's reckoning.' (Betz 1986: 53fn).

In the core myth of Egyptian religion, the god Osiris is also dismembered into fourteen parts, each corresponding with a lunar day. The changes in gender of the sacrificial victim may have hidden the fact that the two myths, Egyptian and Tantrik are closely related.[1]

The dismemberment and reassembling of Osiris takes twenty eight days or one lunar month. Here we are being shown a pattern that corresponds with the physical geography. Perhaps it took a month for the Nile floods to subside after the annual inundation that was the physical destruction of the earth god Osiris. As above so below. The body too has a twenty eight day cycle, or if you are a tantrik, it can acquire one. Indian erotic texts like the Ananga Ranga described the movement of sensation across the surface of the skin. These are known in the west as erogenous zones. The early Hindu eroticists only really observed women and described a twenty eight day cycle. In Sanskrit these things are called *candrakala*, phases of the moon.

Many years ago I was shown a manuscript by someone called *Sandolphon*. In the Tankhem tarot, there are twenty-eight major images, not twenty two as in the standard kabalistic deck. Twenty-eight makes a lot of sense. It is a complete circle. You may be wondering what are the extra cards. I can tell you first that the planets correspond not with one card but with four, that is to say four times seven sacred planets. Each planet therefore has four aspects. If you study this you will find it makes a lot of sense.

It is also prefigured in the Tarot created on the astral by the poet and initiate of the Hermetic Order of the Golden Dawn - W.B. Yeats. This tarot currently has no complete earthly manifestations but it is described in his books.

In the Hindu tantrik tradition the first pitha is the only one still currently active and is at Kamarupa in Assam. As its name suggests, it is the place where the yoni of the goddess fell. Kamarupa represents the eastern quarter. The second pitha is known as Purnagiri; it lies in the south, its actual location undecided, and represents the left nipple or sometimes the navel. The third pitha is Uddiyana (the garden), situated in north-west India, in Kashmir, and can be attributed to the right nipple or sometimes the throat. Uddiyana is also the name of an important Bandha used to control the vital breath. The fourth is Arvudama, in Jalandhara in East Punjab, representing the tongue.

Jan Fries has written in his book *Seidways*, about the mystical significance of dismemberment. Dismemberment is a recurring theme in magical traditions. It also occurs in non-literate cultures broadly termed shamanic. I recently talked with Jan about the possibility that alchemy is also based on the myth of dismemberment. The alchemist's body is 'dismembered' at a microscopic level by the bio-genic substances and drugs he or she has made. Alchemists are often said to immerse themselves in a cauldron for this purpose or to take 'shiva's semen' or the like, whose formula is a closely guarded secret. The result is described as catastrophic as the body almost dies and begins to fall apart. If the operation is successful a new or revivified body emerges.

Western alchemy is probably not as reliable a source as the eastern texts, which have not been so heavily edited by two thousand years of Christian interference (what else is Osiris to do with his time).

Breath control was an important metaphor and probably technique, within the Egyptian magical tradition. An important stele shows the gods Seth and Horus in harmony. The plants shown with them are probably ritual psychoactives. Their feet are resting on a windpipe and lungs, said to represent the principle of equipoise.

Bharati suggests that 'the association of the limbs of the sadhaka, or magician, with certain localities may have given rise to the belief regarding particular limbs of the mother goddess.'[2] A characteristic feature of Tantrik rites is the use of the hands to energize parts of the body by 'installing' corresponding images of gods and goddesses, whilst intoning the appropriate power mantra. The name for this technique is *nyasa*.

The 'hand' is the term used to designate the goddess who helps Amon to create the remaining parts of creation by an act of masturbation - or sexual magick. Amon is the Baphometic goat or Goat of Mendes, a glyph very common in magical symbolism.

The distinguished scholar Sircar hints that the section of the myth added by the medieval tantriks was Greek or Egyptian in origin. I have spoken much of the migration of ideas from India to the west into Europe and beyond, and east into China. But this transmission went two ways. This is most obvious when you look at the history of astrology in India, which is clearly derived from Greek, Babylonian and Egyptian sources. The myth of the murder and dismembering of the God Osiris by Seth is one that could have been known in India from Greek sources. The sacred cult centres of ancient Egypt are reputed to have originated in this act, as Isis traversed the landscape searching for the discarded limbs of her beloved Osiris; the phallus was lost for ever, eaten by the Oxyrhynchus fish, the oasis of Oxyrhynchus being a cult centre of the God Seth.

The Egyptian myth of the Oxyrhynchus fish is a close parallel to a tantrik story of a scroll containing forbidden knowledge. In the Indian tradition this was swallowed by a fish, or sometimes overheard by a human temporarily transformed into a fish, which amounts to the same thing. The fish is eventually caught and the scroll discovered by a fisherman. This fisherman is to be

Matsyendranath, the first guru of the Nath sect of Hindu tantriks. Thus is there an ebb and flow - human to god; temple to human.

Hindu temple architecture is completely permeated by geomantic ideas. The basic ground plan of a temple is a stylized picture of the human form called a mandala. A temple is therefore commensurate with a living organism and the holy of holies is called a *garbha*, literally a womb or sexual organ.

An important alternative to physical pilgrimage is the internal variety developed and widely used by tantrik magicians. As Mircea Eliade put it in *Yoga, Immorality and Freedom*, the tantriks absorbed and systematized certain cosmic/natural ideas, so that they become reified within the body. Later on the same ideas are re-imposed on nature with startling effects. The human body corresponds to and is even identical with the universe. The body is often described as the cosmic mount Meru - the axis mundi or even as a tree, whose seed is to be found in the heart. The details of all this are too many and complicated - as is indeed the world - to go into here but the principle is an absolutely crucial one for the tantrik whose ritual almost always makes use of this image which is installed within the body by ritual gestures (*nyasa*). The most widely known version is found in Kundalini Yoga; although I say widely known, it is remarkable how often this well documented system is completely misunderstood. The central Nadi or yogic duct 'susumna' is to be likened to the world mountain; the two lateral ducts at the left and right (Ida and Pingala) to sacred rivers. Ida, which according to the *Kularnava Tantra* (15.35ff) connects with another lunar number sixteen and is the Ganges. Pingala, according to the same source, connects with the solar number twelve and represents the Yamuna river.

The long term project for the friends of the Tankhem (and Hamsa) zonule, would be the exploration of the meta-psychical temple alluded to above. Beginners need first to acquire the mental and ritual skills needed to do this kind of work efficiently. This work is useful whatever the type of magick you choose to do. More advanced work may involve acquisition of the magical temple. Those who favour eastern styles may use the kind of Hindu temple design found in a chapter of Katon Shual's *Sexual Magick* in the chapter on Kundalini. Those with other tastes might prefer to work on another temple that of Seti I. One future aim would be to recover the images for the twenty eight *phases of the moon* or perhaps also known as *The Book of Thoth*. Thoth is also a moon god and has an interesting parentage. My first exploration of the Seti temple gave a brief encounter with Amon, and as I write this I think that Amon would make an interesting first phase corresponding with English letter A. I am also reminded of the story of Vyasa, the bard who composed the *Mahabharata*. He plays a part in the story as well as narrating it and his own story is told first. It contains a reference to 'the joyous outpouring of seed'.

In a later part I will try to describe why I think the temple (and tomb) of Seti I is important. And also why Thelemites in the 'Aeon of Horus', should perhaps value Seth over him.

Some Egyptian Material

What else is a temple but a representation, in material, of the cosmology of the people who built it? I learned this from many years of study of Hindu temples. In my book *Sexual Magick*, I reproduce the ground plan of a common type of Hindu temple, modeled on a human figure, seated in the lotus position. The ancient Hindus, who, in my opinion, represent a continuation of the magical current set in motion by the Egyptians, thought of their temples as microcosmic. Through this idea we can forge a link with the *myth* of the origin of the tarot. The temple represents the archeology of gnosis - the sequence of a journey through the temple represents the initiatory journey to the 'City of the Pyramids'. This theory can be backed up by scholarly research and was first adumbrated by the Egyptologist Siegfried Schott (see bibliography).[3]

The Temple of Seti I is one of the finest designs in the whole of ancient Egypt. There is a stele, found at Abydos, that refers to a place called the 'Stairway to the Gods' which may be an as yet undiscovered natural phenomenon. Alternatively, given its step like structure, the stairway could be the Temple of Seti I. It is full of magical knowledge if you know how to decode it. In the short time I have been studying this temple, numerous important pieces of information and synchronicities have befallen me. I feel encouraged to proceed. It will perhaps take a whole book to lay before the reader all of the relevant sources I have found, but I must make a start.

In many cases I am going to reproduce the words of Omm Sety ('The mother of Sety') not an ancient Egyptian but a woman of our own times, born in 1904, died in 1981 (The year OGDOS was founded).

The following extracts are taken from *Omm Sety's Abydos* courtesy of Benben Publications, Society for the Study of Egyptian Antiquities Studies.

'Autobiography: 'A Fall that Led to Abydos'

I was born in London, England in 1904, and was christened Dorothy Louise Eady. My father was then a Master Taylor, but later switched over to the cinema industry. Neither he nor my mother had any interest in Egypt, ancient or modern.

When I was three years old, I fell down a long flight of stairs and was knocked unconscious. The doctor was called; he examined me thoroughly and pronounced me dead. About an hour later he returned with my death certificate and a nurse to 'lay out the body', but to his astonishment, the 'body' was completely conscious, playing about, and showing no signs of anything amiss! Soon after this accident I began to dream of a huge and lovely building (which I later found out was actually the Temple of Sety I at Abydos). On waking, I would cry bitterly and beg to be allowed to go home. This longing to 'go home' became a joke in the family, and I was assured that I was at home, but I was equally sure I was not.

When I was four years old I was taken to the British Museum in London as part of a family party. Mother said I paid no attention to anything until we reached the Egyptian Galleries. Then I went simple crazy, running about and kissing the feet of all the statues that I could reach. When the family were ready to leave, Mother said I clung to a glass case containing a mummy and screamed, 'Leave me here, these are my people'. She was so surprised that she never forgot the incident.

When I was six years old I saw a picture of the Temple of Sety I at Abydos, in a magazine. I recognized it at once as the place I had always dreamed about, but was puzzled because the photo showed it to be somewhat ruined. I showed the picture to my father, told him it was my home, and that I wanted to return there. Of course, he told me not to talk nonsense. He told me that it was an old temple in a country called Egypt, and that I had never been there in my life.

When I started to go to school, I was bored to tears unless there was a lesson in which there was any reference to Egypt. So I got the bright idea of skipping school and going to the British Museum instead. Old Sir Ernest Budge, who was then Keeper of the Egyptian Collections, saw me nearly every day mooning around the Egyptian Galleries, asked me why I did not go to the school. I replied that the school did not teach me what I wanted to know; I wanted to learn hieroglyphs. So he offered to teach me, and did so.

Then came World War I, and because of the air-raids over the London, the British Museum was closed. I was sent to my Granny's farm in Sussex. There I regularly rode a large white horse (which I named Mut-hotep, after one of the favourite horses of Ramesses II) to the nearest town, Eastbourne, to borrow books on Egypt from the Public Library. So it went on, through the remainder of my childhood, through adolescence - always reading and studying ancient Egypt.

When I was 27 years old I went to work for a small organization run by some Egyptians whose aim was to publish a kind of public relations magazine, explaining the Egyptians to the English reader. While there, I met a young Egyptian who was on a short visit to London to study English educational methods. We exchanged addresses and for a year corresponded regularly. Finally, he wrote and asked me to marry him, enclosing a group photo of his family, decent upper middle-class people. I accepted but my parents refused. However, as I was over age, they could not stop me. Of course, I do not wonder that they refused. They were then living in Plymouth, Devon and had not met my future husband.

So in 1933 I set off for 'home'. When I landed at Port Said, I knelt down, kissed the ground, and swore that I would never leave Egypt - a vow which I have willingly kept.

I was warmly welcomed by my new family and I settled down to *try* to be a good housewife. My poor anxious parents came out to visit us and when they met my husband they were charmed by him. In fact, Mother said that he was much too good for me. He, poor fellow, got the same idea, and after two years he got fed up with my haphazard housekeeping, really awful cooking, and passion for ancient Egypt. He decided to divorce me and marry his cousin, a nice girl who was a good cook and did *not* like antiquities. In the meanwhile I had produced our little son, whom I insisted on naming Sety, after my beloved Pharaoh. That is why the people here call me 'Omm Sety', meaning 'Mother of Sety'. Among the peasants, it is considered very impolite to call a married woman by her real name and so they refer to her as the mother of whoever is her eldest child.

After my divorce, I went to work for the Egyptian Department of Antiquities, first with Prof. Selim Hassan, who was excavating some tombs in the necropolis surrounding the Pyramids of Giza. It was a wonderful and rewarding experience, and I count myself favoured for having worked for such a brilliant and kindly man.

After Prof. Selim Hassan retired, I worked for Dr. Ahmed Fakhry at Dahshur, and again I was lucky in finding a wise and considerate boss. But in spite of the interesting work and kind treatment, my heart was set on Abydos. Since for many years my aim had been to work, live, die and be buried in Abydos, I had, of course, already been there on pilgrimage to the ancient Holy City. After Dr. Fakhry finished his work at Dahshur, he offered me the choice of a well-paid, comfortable job in the Records Office in Cairo, or a not well-paid and somewhat physically hard job in Abydos. Needless to say, I chose the latter! So in 1956 the first part of my dream came true.

The Temple of Sety I was then undergoing restoration and I was given over 2000 inscribed fragments of stone to catalogue, fit together and translate the inscriptions. The job took 2½ years.

I bought a small house on the edge of the cultivated land near the Temple. In 1969 I reached the official retiring age of 65 years, so the Antiquities Dept, gave me a small pension and 'turned the old mare out to pasture.' I have a tomb prepared in my garden, in the ancient style and am now waiting for the second half of my wish to come true - to die and be buried here.

In the meantime, I am enjoying life, I have some very good friends in the village, seven cats, and a polite cobra who comes and goes as the fancy moves him. I consider myself to be a very lucky woman, and give heartfelt thanks to the ancient gods who heard my prayers and brought me home.

Omm Sety, Abydos, May 1979

Abydos, The Holy City
Introduction

Since long past ages, and in all parts of the world, there have existed sacred cities or places, to which devotees of various religions have made pilgrimages - Mecca, Jerusalem, Benares and Rome, to mention just a few of them. However, the oldest of such holy places of which we have concrete evidence is Abydos in Upper Egypt. From scenes and inscriptions dating back to the age of the Pyramid builders (about 2700BC), we know that all worshippers of the god Osiris were expected to make a pilgrimage to Abydos to visit the most sacred tomb of their god, who had been worshipped there since even earlier times.

The ancient name of this Holy City was Ab-du, which means 'The Desired Mountain'. And Abydos is a Greek corruption of this name; its modern Arabic name is Arabet Abydos. Until recently the modern name was Arabet el Madfouna, which means 'The Buried Arabia'. Abydos was originally the necropolis of the nearby town of Thinis, the capital of Upper Egypt and the kings of the first and second dynasties had their mud-brick tombs there.

In very primitive times Egypt was divided into several petty kingdoms, each with its own ruler and its own local god. In the course of time these small kingdoms became amalgamated into two large kingdoms, Upper and Lower Egypt. In about 3200BC Mena-Narmer, King of Upper Egypt, made war on his northern rival, conquered him, and united the two halves of the country into one whole. Thus he became the founder of what Egyptologists call the First Dynasty.

For political reasons, Mena decided to build a new capital city at the apex of the Delta, a city later to become famous under the name of Memphis (a little to the south of Cairo).

For the same reason, Mena and his successors built two tombs for themselves, one at Abydos and another at Sakkara, the necropolis is Memphis, the latter probably being cenotaphs.

In those far-off days, Abydos was only a small hamlet housing the priests attached to the royal funerary cults, and to the service of a local god called Khenti-Amentiu. With the rise and spread of the cult of Osiris, and the institution of the pilgrimage, Abydos prospered and eventually became a large and important city. Its downfall came with the enforced abolition of the ancient religion in about 565AD; and today Abydos consist of three small villages; Beni Mansour on the north, Arabet Abydos (which is the most important) and Ghabat, on the south.'

The *Sem* priests wore leopard skin tunics during rituals. They are habitually shown grasping the lower paw of the pelt. It strikes me that this is another instance where magical practice tends to hark back to earlier, more primeval days. These same priests are also shown with a particular hair-knot, which is they are still technically in the child stage of life - ie. Like the Brahmacharin status of Hindu priests. Unlike the Hindu priests, there is also a possible element of taboo breaking in the wearing of animal skins in the temple. The leopard's spots are said to be one of the marks of Seth, branded as a criminal for his murder of Osiris.

What follows is a fairly orthodox account of the Osiris myth that nevertheless succeeds in exposing some of the ancient seasonal myth cycle. See for example the eight festivals of contemporary paganism or the Canaanite myth of Baal as recounted in Gaster. This account is, of course, that of the victors in some ancient theological struggle. It is our intention to restore the myth to its full form.

The God Osiris

You may wonder why so much attention is about to be given to Osiris - considered by some as an old aeon deity? However, whatever way you look at it, Osiris is an important part of the topocosm and always will be. It is my working hypothesis that by deconstructing the primary centre of the Osiris myth, that the true nature of Seth and his journey will also be revealed.

'As Abydos is so closely linked with the cult of the god Osiris, It is better, before going any further, to mention what is now known about that god. The standard version of his story, as it was known during the New Kingdom, was that Osiris, his two brothers Seth and Horus the Elder, and his sisters Isis and Nepthys were all children of Nuit,

Goddess of the Sky, and Geb, God of the Earth. Osiris married Isis and Seth married Nepthys.'

[The Egyptian believed that when] 'Osiris became King of Egypt, the Egyptians were a totally uncivilized people. They lived in temporary settlements along the edge of the desert, dressed in the skins of wild beasts, and lived by hunting and herding wild cattle. They also indulged in human sacrifice and cannibalism.

Osiris taught his subjects the arts of agriculture and irrigation. He showed them how to build houses of sun-dried brick and erect temples of the same material so that they came to live together in harmony in settled communities. Osiris gave them laws and education and even the skill of writing, using the hieroglyphic script invented by his friend, the wise god, Thoth.'

Sun-dried bricks remained the standard material for all domestic architecture in Egypt until the 19th century and is still used in all the villages. They were also used in parts of the temple, perhaps for convenience but maybe also for symbolic reasons connected with the past. Thoth, let me remind you, is the son of Seth and bears a striking resemblance to his father.

'The goddess Isis helped her husband in every possible way. She persuaded the people to cultivate flax and taught the women how to spin thread and weave cloth so that they could wear clean garments of linen instead of animal skins.

Both Osiris and Isis were dearly loved by their subjects. But their evil (sic) brother Seth hated Osiris and was bitterly jealous of his popularity with the people. Seth finally managed to pick a quarrel with Osiris, murdered him, and cut his body into fourteen pieces which he scattered all over Egypt.' [The symbolism of the number fourteen will recur. It is, as I explained earlier, part of the lunar mysteries of this cult.]

'As soon as she heard of this tragedy, Isis set out to search for the fragments of her husband's body, embalmed them with the help of the god Anubis, and buried them in the spot in which they were found. Another tradition says that Anubis and Isis assembled the embalmed fragments and buried them at Abydos. In the oldest versions of the story, which are found in the Pyramid texts, and date from the fifth Dynasty, it is merely stated that Seth murdered Osiris at Abydos and left his body lying on the bank of the canal. It was found by Isis and Nephthys, embalmed by Anubis and buried at Abydos.'

It is interesting that a Jackal god, more renowned for eating corpses than embalming should be synthesized in the cult here. The earliest ancient tombs were even shaped like Anubis's body with the corpse lying in his belly. Could it be, that the early hunter-gatherers practiced sky burial, leaving the corpses in special enclosures in the desert for that sole purpose? The remains of this massive enclosures can still be seen a few mile from Abydos.

According to this version of the story, the head of Osiris was buried at Abydos. The heart was buried on the Island of Philae, near Aswan. The phallus was thrown into the Nile and was swallowed by a fish. For this reason the eating of fish was forbidden to the priests. A similar taboo exists in India and in Tantrism the taboo is reversed and the eating of fish is one of the five powerful enjoyments or Makaras. Note that the murder of Osiris actually takes place at Abydos, perhaps on the banks of old channel of the Nile that runs in front of the Temple of Seti I but is now dry. The official standard of the city of Abydos represents the head of Osiris on a stake

'At the time of his murder, Osiris and Isis had no children but by mystical means, Osiris achieved a physical resurrection for one night and slept with Isis. By this means she conceived her son, Horus, who was later to avenge his father's death.

Seth seized the throne of Egypt and ruled as a despotic tyrant. Isis fled away to the north where she hid herself in the vast marshes of the Delta to await the birth of her son, Horus. She was joined by her sister Nepthys who, horrified by the crimes of Seth, left him forever.

When Horus had grown to manhood, he challenged the right of his evil uncle to the throne and after many legal battles, actual wars and trials of strength, eventually overcame him, avenged the murder of Osiris and regained the throne of Egypt. Horus ruled Egypt in the same high traditions as his father Osiris and became the type of the perfect Pharaoh. In fact, until the end of the Pharaonic period, all the rulers used the name of Horus as one of their official titles.

Some scholars think that the cult of Osiris originated in the Delta and that he was identified with a god named Andjty who was worshipped at Busiris (now Abusir el Malek). But it seems more likely that the opposite is true, because Osiris has always been represented as wearing the white crown of Upper Egypt and never the Red Crown of the North. There are others who believe that the story of Osiris contains a kernel of truth, and that he was an actual historical character, but when he actually lived cannot, up to now, be proved. In the writer's opinion, there is a possibility that Osiris and Narmer-Mena are the same person. For one thing, the people of Egypt before the first dynasty were a primitive people, but with the founding of that dynasty by Narmer-Mena, the Egyptian civilization sprung full-blown, yet purely Egyptian in character; it was not a foreign importation. Tradition says that Narmer-Mena was killed by a hippopotamus; Osiris was murdered by Seth, who sometimes took the form of a hippopotamus, as shown in the reliefs at Edfu Temple. Narmer-Mena was succeeded by his son, Hor-sha. The later had two tombs, one at Abydos and another that seems to have been a cenotaph, at Sakkara. In this, Prof. Walter Emery found an alabaster vase, inscribed 'Hor-sha the son of Isis', the only example of a pharaoh bearing this titles. The name 'Hor-sha' means 'Horus the warrior'. So as the person later to be worshipped as the god Horus was indeed the son of Isis and was also a warrior, one cannot help wondering; it seems to be more than a mere coincidence. Furthermore, an ivory label found in the tomb of Hor-sha at Abydos shows him performing a ceremony in front of Narmer-Mena, who is clad in the traditional costume of Osiris!'

'Omm Sety's theory, was rejected by most Egyptologists, although the process by which historical characters were in later times regarded as ancient deities is fairly well documented in ancient Egypt and indeed elsewhere. There is another theory that the ancient methods of killing the moribund pharaoh (Heb-Seb), was by the use of a wild hippopotamus. The Heb-Sed festival fell on the thirtieth Jubilee year of the King. He had to run a race and if he failed he was killed and replaced. Some believe this is the origin of the motif of ritual kingship and indeed because of the time period the whole notion of the 'Saturn return'. This rite was replaced by symbolic race. (P.35 Omm Seti's Abydos). I myself had a vision in which an old King was killed in the Osirion, which has a water channel and connection to the Nile, perhaps for this purpose. In other words, Narmer-Mena may have been reenacting a much older custom. It is in the belly of Seth that the deceased 'king' is taken to the underworld, as was later depicted on the walls of the restored Osirion. This is another important metaphor from the ancient Near-East. '

'Osiris was, mankind is indebted to him for a decent, orderly way of life, a firm promise of resurrection and everlasting life, and a creed that made man responsible for his behaviour. For tradition says that because of his goodness on earth, the Great God (whom the Egyptians called 'Lord of All') appointed him to be kind and Judge in the Other world. Each person after death had to enter the great Judgment Hall where, in the presence of Osiris, his heart, symbolizing his conscience, was weighed in a balance against an ostrich plume, emblem of absolute Truth and justice. At the same time, the deceased must be able to deny committing 42 sins, and if his denial is false, his heart will speak up and contradict him. Whatever the outcome of the judgment, it was Osiris who meted out the reward or punishment. If the deceased was innocent, Osiris would grant him a place in his kingdom, Amenti (which means 'The West') was a replica of the earthly Egypt he loved so well. If the deceased was guilty, he was banished to a place closely resembling the Christian idea of Hell. There was no mercy, no death-bed repentance in the cult of Osiris; but the god in his wisdom, and remembering his own life on earth, took account of the reasons that led the deceased into sin and decreed a light or heavy punishment accordingly.'

This whole scenario lends itself to several different contemporary interpretations, including a shamanic ordeal to be encountered in this life, not necessarily post mortem. The above account also shows that the ancient Egyptians were closer to the Hindu idea of Karma than they were to Christian sin. Of course the Tantrik ideal is to avoid Karma. If you have committed a supposed sin, it is not possible to change that state of affairs. It is, however, possible to alter how you *feel* about that event. The essence of the ordeal in the Judgment Hall of Osiris seems about how clear your conscience is - not whether you have done this or that 'bad' act. Part of the function of Seth's journey is deconditioning, so that you feel fully reconciled to those acts that are part of your humanity. Other ancient versions of the myth omit the 'negative confession' altogether.

'So Abydos has the honour of being the birthplace of this cult that later spread all over Egypt, and in Roman times was carried all over Europe, even reaching the misty isle of Britain, the existence of which the Egyptians had never dreamed.

A Brief History of Abydos

As the Egyptians did not have a fixed dating system, it is, with few exceptions, difficult to assign an exact date to a period or event. They dated events, monuments, etc., to the year of the reign of each king. Thus, we know the length of each reign only by its last dated monument; in other words its minimum length.

Approximately 4000BC[7]Abydos was a small hamlet inhabited by priests who served the royal tombs of the Thinite kings of the first and second dynasty, and the small temple of the local god, Khenti-Amentiu, whose name means 'President of the Westerners', the 'Westerners' being a synonym for the dead. The modest temple of this god was built of sun-dried bricks and consisted of only three chapels and a small courtyard. With the deification of Osiris as ruler and judge of the Dead, he also was called 'President of the Westerners' and it was not long before the earlier god was fully absorbed and identified with him.

Abydos in the Old Kingdom (About 2723BC - 2475BC.)

With the rise of the cult of Osiris, Abydos began to grow in size and fame. The old temple of Khenti-Amentiu had been enlarged, now in stone masonry; its site was in the great enclosure, now known as Kom el Sultan (The Sultan's Mound). Here Prof. Flinders Petrie found what is still the only portrait that we have of King Khufu (Cheops), the builder of the Great Pyramid. It is a small statuette of ivory, only about three inches high, but so forcefully carved that the minute face fully expresses the iron will and determination of the man who reared a veritable mountain of accurately aligned and fitted masonry. The mysterious building, now known as the Osirion, probably dates to the Fourth Dynasty.

By the time of the Fifth Dynasty, Abydos had become so holy that King Nefer-ir-kar-ra passed a royal decree forbidding any priest or lay workers attached to the temples and necropolis to be removed from their posts, and put out to work in any other place. Any governor or high official who would infringe this law should have all his personal property confiscated and the offender himself consigned to the temple workhouse, to be employed in any hard, forced labour. This decree, engraved on stone, was found by Prof. Petrie while he was excavating in Kom el Sultan.

Abydos in the Sixth Dynasty

By the time of the Sixth Dynasty, Abydos had become one of the most important cult centres in Egypt. Long since the goal of an obligatory pilgrimage, it is now also a favoured place of burial for private persons, the chief centre for the worship of Osiris, and the reputed site of his burial.

Pepy II, who came to the throne at the age of seven years, and ruled for ninety years, took a great interest in Abydos. He rebuilt the ancient temple on a larger and grander scale. He also made a monumental gate of limestone in its temenos wall [that which delineates a sacred enclosure], and this is still standing.

Abydos during the First Intermediate period

Following the death of the aged King Pepy II, there was a complete break-up of the central government and a period of anarchy, now called the First Intermediate Period. No doubt Abydos, as the rest of the country, suffered during this time. General poverty as well as insecurity of travel would have reduced the number of pilgrims, yet, while no great monuments were now being built, several good tombs from the period are known.

It is towards the end of the First Intermediate Period hat we get the first recorded example of the 'Curse of the Pharaohs'; King Khati of the Tenth Dynasty, who was one of the many petty rulers who had divided Egypt up among themselves, became ambitious. Apparently he had overcome most of his rivals and annexed their 'Kingdoms', and then turned his attention to the powerful prince of the Theban House, whose territory extended a little to the north of Abydos. A fierce battle took place in Abydos, during which some of the tombs were damaged. Following this, King Khati suffered some misfortune, and in a document addressed to his son, King Merikara II, he attributes his troubles to the desecration of the tombs, and says: 'Egypt fights in the cemetery, smashing the tombs. Thus did I myself, and the same happened as was done to one who transgresses against the way of the god. The town of Thinis, which was the southern boundary, I captured it like a water-flood. Be long-suffering in ruling that country, act wisely, having regard to the future.'

Abydos during the Middle Kingdom

Egypt gradually emerged from her period of chaos and eventually a powerful ruler from Thebes, Amenemhat I, seized control of the entire country and founded the XIIth Dynasty (2013-1785BC), one of the most glorious periods of Egyptian history.

By now the importance of Abydos was fully and finally established. The ancient temple at Kom el Sultan, cradle of the cult of Osiris, was enlarged and embellished and a new necropolis of private tombs and cenotaphs sprang up in its vicinity. The Temple of Osiris was entirely renewed by Amenemhat II (1849 - 1801 BC) and was surrounded by an immense temenos wall of mud brick. Influential persons were permitted to erect memorial stele or statues within this sacred enclosure.

From this period also we know for certain that the famous 'Mystery Play' of Osiris was being performed at Abydos. This, the oldest drama yet known, was performed during the annual pilgrimage. It consisted of seven episodes in the life, death and resurrection of Osiris, each episode taking place on a separate day. The king, or his deputy, played the part of the god Horus and other deities were played by the priest and priestesses of Osiris. The women playing the parts of Isis and Nepthys were traditionally supposed to be virgins, but as most of the priestesses were married, this may have presented a problem. Curiously enough, the part of Osiris was never played by a living man; he was impersonated by a life sized, jointed wooden statue. This reluctance to portray a divine personage by a human actor has persisted until modern times.'

With very little modification the ritual drama described by Omm Sety could be compared with the eight sabbaths of contemporary witchcraft, which may owe their existence to the work of Egyptologist Margaret Murray in collaboration with Gerald Gardner. According to folklorist Theodor Gaster, they may also be the origin of 'Punch and Judy' and the mummer's play. Omm Sety now goes on to describe was known anciently as Pega the Gap, supposedly the route through which the souls of the dead made their way to Amenti, the Kingdom of Osiris, and through which they would return to re-visit Abydos on the occasion of the Feast of Osiris.

'At this time also, the sacred tomb of Osiris, the goal of the pilgrimage, was said to be at the western edge of the plain, near the gap in the mountains. In reality this was the mud-brick mastaba of King Djer of the 1st Dynasty. It appears that the archaic writing of this king's name was confused with Khenti-Amentiu, which was now one of the epithets of Osiris. It was to this tomb that all the pilgrims came, bearing offering of food and drink in earthenware or alabaster vessels. In the course of time, a veritable mountain of offering pots covered the whole area surrounding the tomb, and remains to this day. It is now known as Omm el Gaab, which means 'Mother of Potsherds'. It is still possible to find small, complete cups, and the modern local children believe that these are made by 'afreet' (ghosts) on a Wednesday, baked on a Thursday and may be found on a Friday morning. But after noon on Friday, no more will be found until the following week!

But there were secular as well as religious reasons why Abydos flourished during the XIIth Dynasty. Then, as until quite recently, the main route to the oases of Kharga and Dahleh in the western desert, lay close to Abydos, and government officials travelling this route on state business usually took the opportunity of making their pilgrimage to the holy city, and erecting a monument there to commemorate the event. The kings also were now making cenotaphs for themselves in Abydos. Senusert III (1887 - 1849 BC) built a splendid tomb and mortuary chapel at the southern end of the necropolis. This was clearly a cenotaph, as he was actually buried in a large brick pyramid at Dahshur, south of Sakkara. Two monuments from this cenotaph suffered rather undignified fates in modern times. One is a naos in crystalline limestone in which is seated a life-sized statue of the king. The local people dragged it to the edge of the desert, laid it on its back, and filled it with water for use as a cattle drinking trough! Perhaps not so inappropriate for a worshipper of the Apis bull. However, the Egyptian Department of Antiquities stepped in and rescued poor King Senusert from his ignominious fate! Cleaned and set upright, he now graces the second court of the Temple of Seti I.

The other monument is the lower half of what was once a very fine seated statue of King Senusert. The upper part, from the waist, is missing but the lower half and the throne on which he is seated is intact. Somehow or other, his majesty has gained a reputation for solving problems of infertility, and it is not uncommon sight to see would be mothers seated hopefully on the royal lap, Curiously enough, it often works! Which shows how ancient a tradition of folk reverence can be.

Abydos during the second intermediate period

The Kings of the XIIIth Dynasty were a far different type from the wise and powerful rulers of the previous royal house. King Nefer-hotep was a well-meaning soul, and he decided to have a new statue of Osiris made for the old temple at Kom el Sultan. In order to be sure that the statue was correctly fashioned according to the ancient tradition, he went personally to the library of the great temple of Heliopolis, where there was a papyrus roll setting forth precise specifications for the construction of the various divine statues. He also personally supervised the fashioning of the statue.

It was not long before internal political disputes and struggles began to take place and taking advantage of Egypt's weakness, a hoard of Asiatic nomads invaded the country and made themselves masters of the delta and middle Egypt. They were called the Hyksos and their rule was a disaster for the country. Their domination lasted for about 150 years, and during that time the monuments were destroyed, the tombs plundered and the people persecuted. Eventually one of the princes of the old royal house of Thebes gathered enough supporters to raise an open rebellion against the Hyksos, and after many fierce battles finally defeated then, drove them out of Egypt into western Asia, where they were finally completely wiped out from the face of the earth.

However, Hyksos domination never extended so far south as Abydos, which had quietly continued on its own peaceful way. Certainly no great monument had been built there during this period, and far fewer pilgrims were able to come and pay homage to their beloved god, Osiris. Nevertheless his cult continued to flourish, and people were still building their modest tombs and cenotaphs in the sacred necropolis.

Ahmes I (1580-1557BC) the heroic king who had finally driven the Hyksos out of Egypt, had made for himself a fine rock-cut tomb at Abydos. In order to hide the whereabouts of this tomb, and to protect it against possible plundering, he had all the rock cut from its excavation carted to the edge of the desert, piled into a great heap, and cased with limestone, to form a false pyramid. In this, he played a good joke on posterity, for ancient tomb-robbers and modern archaeologists have spent many fruitless weeks of hard work tunneling through, under and around this 'pyramid' in a frantic search for the non-existent 'burial chamber filled with treasure'. Ahmes also added to the old temple of Osiris at Kom el Sultan and so popular was he in Abydos, that he was deified and his statue was regarded as an oracle.

Abydos during the New Kingdom

Amenhotep I (1557 - 1547 BC) the founder of the glorious XVIIIth dynasty, built monuments in Abydos in honour of his father, the heroic Ahmes I, and his dearly loved grandmother, Queen Teti-sheri. Amenhotep embarked on a project of making millions of mud-bricks for use in the rebuilding and restoring cities devastated by the Hyksos. In this work, it is known that he was employing thousands of Semitic workmen, which suggests that he might have been the pharaoh of the Bible. Many of Amenhotep's successors, the great warrior kings of the XVIIIth dynasty, embellished Abydos, and the massive walls, red granite doorways and thresholds of Thothmes III ('Egypt's Napoleon') may still be seen at Kom el Sultan.

But Abydos received its crowning glory at the beginning of the XIXth Dynasty (1312BC) when Seti I built his wonderful temple of Osiris, a masterpiece of Egyptian art and architecture that annually draws admiring visitors for all parts of the world. Seti also built here a temple on behalf of his father Ramesses I, another temple dedicated to the ancient kings of Egypt, and a small place for his own use which he called 'Heart's Ease in Abydos'. He also restored many of the monuments of his predecessors. Seti's famous son, Ramesses II, also built a temple here in honour of Osiris.

In the XXth dynasty, Ramesses III (1198-1167BC) gave some rich endowments to Abydos. The great Harris Papyrus mentions some of his gifts which included a temple of stone (so far undiscovered) equipped with priests and lay-workers to the number of 844, offering vessels of gold and silver, a new sacred barge of Osiris made of cedar wood, and a statue of himself.

Ramesses IV built a small temple for Osiris a little to the north of that of Ramesses II. Fragments from it have come to light, bearing rather flat and lifeless reliefs. Ramesses IV seems to have been a somewhat overbearing, even impious fellow, and a liar into the bargain. On an inscribed stele which he erected in Abydos, he not only claims to have made more benefactions than he had done in reality, but also he adopted a high-handed, almost bullying tone towards Osiris, demanding rewards for all that he had done. He says to the god: 'You shall give me health, a long life and a prolonged reign, sight to my eyes, hearing to my ears, and pleasure to my heart daily. You shall give me to eat until I am full, and give me to drink until I am drunk, and let my descendants rule as kings in this land for ever and ever. You shall double for me the long reign of Ramesses II, for I have done more for you in my four years of reign than he did in his 67 years'. What a nerve.

Abydos during the Saitic period.
The XXIst dynasty was founded by Heri-Hor, High priest of Amon-ra, who seized power from the weakling Ramesses XII and thus began the disastrous rule of the priest-kings (1090-945BC). These well-meaning blunderers ruled Upper Egypt, with their capital at Thebes, while a family of Libyan origin governed the Delta. A son of one of these latter had a splendid burial at Abydos which still remained the coveted place of burial. But division is weakness and once more Egypt fell prey to foreign intervention.

The XXVIth dynasty (663-525 BC) brought a new period of prosperity and settled government to Egypt, which was again united under the rule of a powerful house. Their capital was at Sais in the Delta, hence the dynasty is usually known as the Saitic Period. At this time there was a tendency to look back to the great 'good old days' of the past and in religion, art and daily life there was a conscious attempt to revive the old styles, traditions and institutions.

Needless to say, this period brought a new prosperity to Abydos. King Ahmes II (the Amasis of Herodotus) (569-525BC) carried out some work there apparently having been prompted by his personal physician, a confirmed lover of the Holy City. The doctor, who rejoiced in the name of Pef-nef-di-Neit, had been on a pilgrimage to Abydos and found things not at all to his liking, Apparently the Governor of Abydos at that time was one of those who believed 'feathering one's own nest'. He had neglected the temples and the fields of the sacred estates. On top of that, he had taken away the free ferry-boat that used to ply between Abydos and the Nile, and took for himself the 'duty' paid on all goods entering the Nile Valley from the oases of the western desert, the 'customs office' being situated in Abydos. All these short-comings Pef-nef-di-Neit reported to King Ahmes, who gave him an order on the treasury (an ancient 'blank cheque') and sent him off to Abydos to put matters right. He performed his task to everyone's satisfaction, except the Governor's! The latter was dismissed from office and all his property confiscated. The funds from the stolen customs duty was now used to build tombs for the poor of Abydos, and the free ferry was again put to its proper use. In recognition of his service, he was permitted the honour of erecting a statue of himself in the court of the temple of Osiris. This statue, which is inscribed with the story of the doctor's exploits, is now in the Louvre in Paris.

During the Saitic Period the cults of the sacred animals began to gain prominence and, at Abydos, there was a large and important canine cemetery. At the Old IInd dynasty enclosure (the original purpose of which is not certain) mummified ibis-birds sacred to the god Thoth, were buried in earthenware jars. The modern name for this enclosure is Shunet el Zebib which means 'the storehouse of raisins'. But this is surely a corruption of the ancient name of Shuna pa Hib, meaning 'the storehouse of the Ibis'.

Abydos during the Graeco-Roman period
The sacred reputation of Abydos was maintained all through the Greco-Roman period (332BC until the Vth century AD). Strabo and other classical writers visited it and recorded its wonders. The beautiful temple of Seti I had gained a reputation for healing, and sick people were allowed to sleep in one of its courts in order that a dream might reveal a remedy for their illnesses. Many returned, cured, to write or scratch on the walls expressions of gratitude for their recovery.'

Prostitution, perhaps of a sacred variety, was well known in the Holy City. Omm Sety tells us that in addition to these graffiti, which were written in Egyptian, there are other in Greek, Phoenician and Aramaic.

'Sad to say not all these scribblers turned their thoughts to sacred matters. One fellow mentions nothing about his recovery from sickness, but left a detailed and glowing account of the anatomical perfections of one of the 'ladies' of Abydos. She must have been a well-known character, because someone else came and wrote underneath the first inscription saying, 'I agree with you, she is everything you say - but to my mind, she is too short.' Human nature does not change much.

Incidentally, the custom of sick persons going to sleep in the sacred places has not yet died out. There are several tombs of Moslem holy men in the neighbourhood of Abydos where sufferers go to pass the night in the hope of a cure, and very often, not in vain.

It was in Roman times that an oracle of the little dwarf god, Bes, appeared in Abydos and became very famous. It was finally prohibited by a Coptic saint named Moses, in the VIth century AD

With the final downfall of the ancient religion, Abydos became for a while a Christian stronghold and several churches and monastic buildings were erected there, often of stones taken from ancient monuments. One of these churches, dedicated to Saint Damiana and Saint Moses, was built in another 2nd dynasty enclosure, a little to the north of Shunet el Zebib. It is still in regular use by the Coptic community in Abydos.

Since the day when a Christian emperor of Rome ordered the burning of the Egyptian temples, the murder of the priests and the pillaging of the sacred treasuries, Egypt - has undergone two changes of national religion. The modern inhabitants of Abydos, simple peasants, know nothing of the ancient religion, yet they and their neighbours for miles around, still come to the temple of Seti and the other monuments, imploring help in their problems from powers whose names they do not know. Abydos has not quite lost its sacred reputation, which it has held for almost 6000years - can any other religious centre in the world rival this claim?

The Temple of Seti I

Having given a very brief outline of the rise and decline of the city of Abydos (cf.JSSEA Vol.X No.1), it is time to consider its most important monuments. Of these, the most famous, beautiful and best-preserved is the Temple of Seti I. It stands on the eastern edge of the desert, and dominates the village of Arabet Abydos. The entire building was completed during the reign of Seti I (1313-1292 BC), as well as all the beautiful bas-relief sculpture. Unfortunately, the decoration of the building was incomplete at the time of the King's death, and so the reliefs on the exterior, and in the first hypostyle hall were carried out by Seti's son and successor, Ramesses II. He filled up all the blank walls with scenes showing himself adoring the gods,

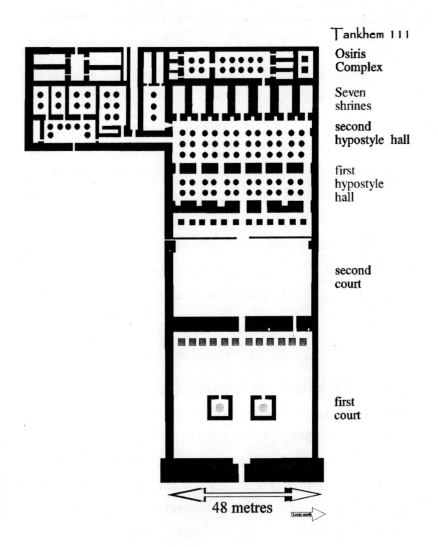

Tankhem 111

Osiris Complex

Seven shrines

second hypostyle hall

first hypostyle hall

second court

first court

48 metres

Local north

and also left long inscriptions on the façade of the temple reminding us what a good boy he was to complete his father's monument!

King Seti I

Before describing the temple, let us have a glimpse of the career of the man responsible for this masterpiece, King Seti I.

The XVIIIth Dynasty, which had begun so gloriously, seemed doomed to end in disaster. Akhenaton, the heretic king, lost the great Egyptian Empire through sheer neglect and his weak and incompetent successors worsened the situation. Fortunately for Egypt, General Horemheb, an upright and far-seeing officer in the army, seized the throne from the corrupt old King Ay, and proclaimed himself King of Upper and Lower Egypt.

Instead of trying the now hopeless task of regaining the Egyptian Empire, Horemheb set to work to set the internal affairs of the country in order. He cleansed the corrupt government, introduced land reforms, and drew up laws for the protection of the falahin. Apparently Horemheb was childless, as he nominated as his successor his friend and brother officer, Ramesses, who had also been acting as his vizier. When Horemheb died in 1315BC, this man ascended the throne as Ramesses I and founded the XIXth dynasty.

Ramesses I, who came of an old established military family living in the eastern Delta, had a son named Seti, also an officer, who before his father's accession had been Commander of the Eastern Frontier garrison in a place now called Kantarah. But on reaching the kingship,

Ramesses I recalled Seti to Thebes, to act as his vizier. But Ramesses was now an elderly man and after a brief reign of two years, he died and was succeeded by Seti. The latter proved to be one of the finest rulers that Egypt has ever known. He completed Horemheb's internal reforms, restored peace and security to the Middle East, built many beautiful monuments, as well as restoring older ones that were falling into decay. He was also a kindly, humane man, thoughtful of the welfare of his meanest subjects. On one occasion, he heard that the conditions of life in a gold mine in the eastern desert were so bad that the workmen (convicts sentenced to hard labour) were dying like flies. Instead of sending an official to investigate the complaint, Seti insisted on going himself. Apparently the situation was very bad, and the men had insufficient supplies of fresh water and food. Seti remedied the situation by having a well dug and vegetable gardens planted. He then made a decree ordering that every man working in the mine should have a daily ration of ten loaves of bread, five bundles of fresh vegetables and two large slices of meat; also *new* clothes twice a month. One hardly expects a king in those far-off times to trouble himself over the welfare of some convicted criminals; one would rather expect the reaction to be, 'They die, so what? Plenty more where they came from.' No wonder some ancient texts say of him, 'you spread yourself in protection over the common people. The youth of the nations - you know their needs, and you supply them.'

A description of the Temple

The temple, enclosed by a vast temenos wall of mud-bricks, occupies a site that slopes from west to east. This meant that it had to be artificially leveled into four steps, rising up from the east, before ever a stone could have been put in place. According to an inscription, Seti was commanded by an oracle to build the temple in this unpromising site.

The main fabric of the building is fine limestone from a quarry in the neighbourhood, with roofing-slabs, architraves, columns and doorways, all parts under great stress, of Nubian sandstone. The plan, instead of being the traditional rectangle, resembles the Roman letter L in reverse. The space between the eastern and southeastern part of the temenos wall and the short 'arm' of the L was occupied by a royal reception hall and twenty magazines. These were all built and paved with mud-brick, but had limestone columns, doorways and window grills.

Immediately to the east of the temple was a quay, built of sandstone, on the banks of the old Nif-wer channel, which once connected Abydos with the Nile.

Then comes a level space, (originally paved), from which a fine stairway leads up to a terrace. This stairway, as most of those in the temple, consists of two sets of steps with sloping treads, and having a ramp between them. It has now been restored on the foundation of the original. The terrace, the front of which was decorated with war-like scenes relating to Ramesses II, supported the massive, but now ruined First Pylon.'

The design of the temple, with its gently slopping stairways and ramps perhaps facilitating long 'snake-like' processions on festival days.

The First Court

'A great doorway in the centre of the pylon (only opened on special occasions) gives access to the First Court, the walls of which were decorated by Ramesses II with scenes of his battles and triumphs. Unfortunately most are badly damaged, but on the south wall, there still remains a large scene of Ramesses returning after a victory, bringing a number of prisoners-of-war. His pet lion runs beside his chariot. On the north wall is a very natural representation of Ramesses about to mount in his chariot; he places one foot on the floor of the car grasps the front rail with both hands, and is about to spring up into the vehicle. In each of the southern and northern walls of the court is a small doorway. The south one opens from a passage between the wall of the temple and that of the magazines and was used for everyday purposes. The door in the north led to the still unexcavated palace of Seti.

On the other side of the main axis of the court are two ablution basins. As these bear inscription dating from the reign of Seti I, it shows that at least part of the temple was in use, in spite of the decoration being still incomplete. Near to the northern ablution basin, is the well that fed them. It still contains water and never grows dry.'

The purifying ritual power of water is a feature of most religions ever since.

'At the western end of the court, another double stairway leads up to a low terrace, on which stood a portico fronting a pylon shaped wall. The roof of the portico was borne by twelve square pillars of limestone and sandstone, but of these only the lower parts remain. On the west wall of the portico (which is the eastern face of the false pylon) Ramesses has recorded the names and figures of some of his many children, The figures of the boys, mostly damaged, are on the southern half of the wall. The girls, who have fared better, are on the northern side, in fact five of them on the north wall are almost perfectly preserved, and very pretty and elegantly dressed girls they are. All have their names inscribed in front of them. The middle one is Tenpitnefert, which means 'Happy Year'. Presumably she was born on New Year's Day! The last one is Merit-neter, 'God loves-her'. Some ancient Egyptian personal names have a somewhat puritan flavour!

The Second Court

On the days when the great central doorway was closed,
access to the second court was through a small door in the
northern end of the false pylon. The wall scenes in this
court have quite a different theme. On the east wall are
shown some more of the royal children, but on the north
and south walls, Ramesses is shown offering to the
different gods. In other words, while in the first court he
brags about his battles and victories, here he is 'behaving
himself', and being nearer to the temple, shows his
religious devotion to the gods.

At the west end of the northern wall is a curious
alteration. The last two religious scenes have been partly
erased and in their place is a gigantic figure of Ramesses.
It was never finished, but seems intended to represent him
binding a captive enemy. Near by is a large stele, built in
one with the wall of the court. On it is a long inscription
recounting all the benefactions that Ramesses made of
the gods of Abydos. A similar stela exists opposite, on the
south wall, near it, is an ancient well.'

It is my hypothesis that the changes to the design of the temple,
made by Ramesses, represented the beginning of a movement
away from Seti's own philosophy. Given what Ramesses put in this
place, (and the kind of rituals that occurred in this part of the
second court) it seems likely to me that the erased images were
relating in some way to the cult of Seth *and* Horus. These are not

the only iconographic changes made by Ramesses and his family. I believe that it was at this time that stone masons were instructed to carefully incise the Seth-animal from the cartouche of Seti. The Seth-animal functions, as a syllabic sign in the script, thus the name of Seti-mer-en-ptah, would be spelt with the Seth animal as the first character. The erasers only missed three examples of the syllable, all in the sanctuary of Amon Ra. You can see an example of their work on a statue of Seti now in the British Museum.

The Second Portico

'At the western end of the second court, a flight of steps, divided as usual by a ramp, ascends to the second portico and the façade of the temple. The roof of the portico (now restored) rests upon twelve rectangular limestone pillars on sandstone bases. They stand six to the north and six to the south of the main entrance to the temple. Each face of every pillar is adorned with a representation, mostly showing Ramesses being embraced by a god or goddess, as well as some depicting the now dead and deified Seti I. On the sides of the pillars flanking the main entrance, we see Ramesses about to enter the temple, On the northern side of the entrance he appears as King of Lower Egypt and wears the Red Crown, while on the southern side he is in his role as King of Upper Egypt and wears the White Crown. In both scenes he wears handsome toe-thong sandals, the front of which turns up in a graceful point. The fact that he is wearing sandals shows that he is supposed

to be still outside the temple, as once inside the holy place of the gods he must go bare-footed.

The western faces of some of the pillars, which were protected by the roof of the portico, still retain much of their original colouring.

On the northern wall of the portico are two large scenes. That to the east, which is outside the roofed part, shows Ramesses symbolically clubbing a bunch of Egypt's Asiatic enemies, who kneel in terror before him. The god Amon-Ra helpfully offers him the curved war-axe. This ceremonial sacrifice of enemies had long ago perhaps been an actual fact, but there is evidence that since at least as early as the XVIIIth Dynasty it was merely symbolic. The prisoners were led in front of the temple, made to kneel and the King lightly tapped them with his mace, and let them go. The poor wretches must have had a few bad moments if they did not understand the nature of the ceremony!

The second scene is under the roof of the portico, and so has retained much of its colouring. It shows Ramesses (still outside) wearing his sandals. He is reciting the offering formula in front of Osiris, an act which will magically provide an inexhaustible supply of food and drink for the god. The same formula was also recited for the dead, and for the same purpose.

At the northern end of the west wall of the portico, which is also a facade of the temple, is a small doorway for everyday use. Next is a very large coloured scene. The gods Horus, and the ram-headed Khnum, take Ramesses by his hands and lead him to the Temple of Ra-Horakhty at Heliopolis. Here he stands before the sacred Tree of Life, and the god writes his name upon the leaves. For every leaf so inscribed the King will rule for one year. As Ramesses reigned sixty-seven years, Ptah had plenty of writing to do.

There is a belief among Moslems in Egypt that in Paradise there is a tree called 'Tree of Destiny', which bears as many leaves as there are people in the world. Each leaf bears the name of each person living, but in the middle of the Arabic month of Shaaban (which is followed by the fasting month of Ramadan), the tree shakes, and the leaves bearing the names of those persons destined to die in the coming year fall down. It has long been the custom for children to gather in groups at sunset on the evening of the fateful day, and go round the streets singing:

'O Lord of the Tree of Destiny, make our leaves strong and green upon its branches. For we, O Lord, are Your little children.'

The vaulted chapel of Amon-ra

The eastern half of the chapel of Amon-ra is rather badly marred by smoke blackening, as well as by wanton damage to the figures, as this chapel was also coloured during King Seti's lifetime. In the first scene of note on the northern wall, Seti, wearing the costume of a ritual priest come to wash the statue of Amon-ra. The god, dignified and stately has his flesh coloured blue, as is usual in his representations. Egyptian religious tradition said that men were created from the tears of the god. The name 'Amon' means 'hidden' or 'mysterious', and the ancient hymns to Amon refer to him as:

'Thou art the One,
Maker of all things that are;
the only One, maker of what has been.
For whose eyes men came forth
at whose word the gods came into being.'
It was also said that no one knew his form.

In the following scene, the god represented is the ithyphallic Min, giver of fertility to man, beasts and crops, but he is referred to as Amon-Ra in the accompanying inscription.

On the upper part of the western end of the southern wall is a beautiful scene showing King Seti burning incense in front of the sacred boat of Amon-Ra. The latter is a truly splendid vessel, its prow and stern adorned with great golden rams' heads, the ram being the sacred animal of Amon-ra. Behind the great boat are two smaller ones belonging to Khonsu, the son of Amon-Ra, and Mut, the wife of Amon-ra. Each boat has a figurehead representing the deity to which it is dedicated.

Immediately below this scene, Seti presents vases of perfume to Amon-Ra. It is interesting to see that the accompanying inscription recording the speech to be uttered during this rite, is taken word for word from the Pyramid texts, written nearly two thousand years earlier.

extracts from Omm Sety ends

——————————————————

The 'three' forms of Ra.

Storytelling can be a useful way of exploring the imaginal world. The presence of an audience, adds the necessary element of dialectic that can be so productive of magical intuition. It was whilst preparing a story for a session that I came upon the following passage, which is so relevant to the shrine of Amon-Ra.

It comes from Margaret Pinch's *Magic in Ancient Egypt* (BM 1994 p. 30-1). It is extracted from the *Turin Magical Papyrus,* which has a long section on charms to cure snake venom.

The same manuscript has a similar story concerning Seth and Horus. Seth is compelled to reveal his true name, and therefore nature. It is also an important point of contact between the Egyptian and Tantrik traditions. The power to deal with deadly snake venom is one of the celebrated abilities of Ayurvedic physicians, a brand of medicine with much in common with Tantrism. See my *Tantra Sadhana* for details about the caste of Matanga sorceresses, whose skills were used by the Buddha to counteract serpent infestation. It is perhaps significant, that the hieroglyph that in the Egyptian language is used to connote 'goddess' is the striking cobra. It may be a coincidence but the same image is worn by Shiva as an earring.

In my rendering of the Egyptian story I have taken the liberty of interpolating an episode from the mythology of Parvati, Lady of the Mountains in the tantrik tradition. She also constructs a magical child from the sweat of her body. .

'Isis was a wise woman who was familiar with millions of gods and spirits. There was nothing in heaven and earth that she did not know, except the secret name of the sun god Ra. Isis decided to find out the name of the highest of the gods. Ra had become old. His limbs trembled and he sometimes dribbled.'

And when Ra dribbled it would often fall to the earth. And Isis, the magician, took the saliva of Ra and hid it in a safe place. Then she began to dance, gently at first, but soon, as the mood of exaltation took hold of her, her movements became more frenetic and soon she was dancing round and round in wild abandon. Her feet beat the earth to keep time. And still she danced, and when she was exhausted, and could dance no more, she stood still, her whole body quivering and shaking with lust and earth energy. Now her whole body was hot to the touch and her skin glistened with her own sweet smelling perfume of sweat. And Isis took her own sweat and put it with the saliva of Ra. And Isis mixed it all with some clay. And out of this clay She made a snake and animated it with her magick. Isis hid the snake near the path taken by Ra each day.'

Ra left his palace to walk through the land. The magick snake bit the highest of the gods and then disappeared. Ra cried out. The gods who were with him asked what had happened. Ra could not answer. He trembled as the venom penetrated his body as the Nile irrigates the land. He was blinded by the poison. Ra could not identify what had poisoned him, so he ordered the deities who were the most skilled at magick to attend him. Isis diagnosed that Ra had been bitten and claimed that she needed to know his name in order to cure him.

Ra told her that he was the god who had created heaven and earth and that it was he who made the Nile rise. Darkness fell when he closed his eyes and it became light when he opened them again. His names were Kephri in the morning, Ra at midday and Atum in the evening. The venom continued to circulate and Isis said that Ra's true name was not contained in what he had told her. The fiery pain became unbearable, so Ra allowed knowledge of his name to pass from his body to hers. Then Isis the great magician, conjured the venom out of Ra.

This is still a secret and is not revealed in manuscripts. Perhaps this is why some invocations say:

'In the name, and in the name and in the secret name of'

Exercise 1

In this ritual the magi takes on the form of Seti, who is in this instance the representative of any human operator in the temple. I have pictures of Seti, carvings and indeed his actual mummified body, one of the finest surviving and still a beautiful thing.

Seti took his name from the god Seth, who was worshipped in Seti's native province. He did not alter this when he moved to the holy city of Abydos. Seth is sometimes seen as the evil opposer, but try to think of him (or her) as a human being. Many of his supposed crimes, as we shall see, are actually very human indeed.

You come to the temple via the river Nile, the floods are over and navigation is possible. A the boat brings you to a small tributary and you must take another ferry, north west of Abu Shusha, provided free of charge by the temple, to take you up to the oasis of Abydos via a very ancient channel called Nif-Wer. The ferry stops at a special jetty and you, along with other pilgrims.

The sacred enclosure of the temple is delineated by a high wall made of mud bricks. This is the temenos of the sacred space. Move through the temenos and towards the eastern front end of the temple proper, the stone built pylons forming a massive ornamental gateway in the Egyptian temple style. The wooden doors of the temple are shut. This is not the normal way to enter the temple, these are ceremonial doors, and are only used on special festival occasions, when the images of the gods inside are brought out through them and paraded on special boats. There are several other entrances into the temple, depending upon your status and experience. But before moving on, take a good look at the face of the pylons. They are decorated with two full size reliefs, representing two apparently opposing principles that the temple aims to reconcile. You may also see the colossal sculptures of gods, representing similar principles, perhaps male and female, spirit and matter, dark and light. If you can see the top of the pylons, you will see seven flags - the hieroglyphic symbol of the gods or *Neters*

Now move on. Your way in is via a small door in the northern wall of the temple, near its corner with the eastern pylon front. There may well be an 'official' stationed here to ensure the correct etiquette is observed, shoes are removed etc. You may also buy special offerings for your devotion, usually a cylindrical loaf of bread and a small clay pot of beer.

Once inside, you see two square ablution basins in the centre of a perfectly square courtyard, open to the sky. Wash yourself, removing any unnecessary associations of your journey. Look around you. Depending upon time of day and season, different part of the relief on the walls will be clearly visible. But in general the images are of Ramesses II and his various achievements in the outer world. For the ancient Egyptians, warfare, expansion of empire and defence of secure borders were pinnacles of earthly achievement. Do not despise this, try to see the essence that lays behind it, and cast in your own idiom, what the equivalent might be. Pause for a while and explore this.

When you are ready, move towards the western wall and the second pylon; from the hot overhead sun (if it is daytime) to the shade of a portico. As you do so, your steps are slowed as you climb a gentle sloping stairway to the next level about five feet higher than the last. Others are here, perhaps passing over some of the fruits of the temple - divination, sacred objects and food, blessed by contact with the holy of holies. Move on beyond this, through the central doorway into the second courtyard. (Some are allowed to sleep in the courtyards, and elsewhere as an aid to dream incubation).

This is similar to the first court, but more refined. You have moved further towards the west and away from the grosser, but still important elements of the spiritual life. There are different images to be seen representing physical achievement but closer to home that those described earlier. They concern such things as the joys and responsibility of family in all its aspects; the outer observances of festivals and religion; the mysteries of water and of the ecology of the river Nile. Pause for a while here and observe the difference in the imagery as the light shifts and changes. Further to the west is another portico. Once again you must climb a small staircase or ramp rising about five feet under the portico. Now you are just outside the temple proper. Only someone pursuing their true will can pass beyond this point. Notice before going any further, the symmetry of some of the images, again remind yourself of opposites that need to be reconciled. Here are images of Horus and Seth, shown in a unified form.

Now take your courage in both hands and move through the central doorway into the dark interior of the temple. You are confused. Everything is dark and you are in a labyrinth or forest of closed papyrus pillars. Strange noises, sights, smells and sounds assail you. Sometime a shaft of light or a flickering flame illuminates a particular image, try to remember this and record its meaning later. For this experiment, stick, as far as possible to the central pathway through the pillars. In front of you are in fact seven vaulted, cave like shrines of equal prominence. Seven is a special number in this system, very special indeed. Your first task is to remind yourself of the origins and thus you keep to the central colonnade, that leads you inexorable and through gentle rising steps to the vaulted shrine of Amun. As you approach the height of the room decreases with every step. Just outside the shrine are two phallic and colossal statues of Min. You must pass between them, acknowledging each day the sexual nature of your being. Before you is the vaulted, womb-like shrine of Amun. The door is locked. An iron bolt, known as the finger of Seth, is held in place by a clay seal. If you think you have the understanding, then break this seal perhaps with the words:

> *'The finger of Seth is withdrawn from the eye of Horus and it is well. The cord is undone from Amon, the sickness is unloosed from the god.'*

Now the doors may be opened and you can look inside. Try to remember your first impressions. The actual form of Amon is unknown, thus his name means *mysterious*. All the historical imagery such as Baphomet, The Goat of Mendes, are metaphors for the creative vortex. Sometime the image is blue to represent more of the mystery. The image is about your own size and will be facing you from an ornamental wooden shrine box. Beyond this image you can see other strange things. There is a diaphanous veil or screen and beyond this the hint of a secret door.

You may wish to make an offering, saying:

> *'I offer what is in my hands'.*

If you have nothing in your hands, then offer your hands, laying them on the god, meaning that you will later do some work on the god's behalf. If you don't feel ready for this, then leave your offering in a niche, that you will find outside the shrine, in the wall between this shrine and the next one. You might consider performing the orthodox function of the priest, then do to the god, what he/she would like. Primarily this means to clean and tidy the shrine, to change the god's clothing and decoration and to leave some food and drink, taking away the previous times offerings (this will be sold to pilgrims in the temple courtyards).

When you have done, sweep the floor as you retreat, obliterating your footprints and close the door, replacing the seal with one of your own that you can remember. When you are ready, either explore a little further as is your will or return the way you came. Mentally repeating the process in reverse .

I suggest that this point of contact with the creative Amun is the basic practice that should be done before moving onto other deeper mysteries. End the ritual as taught, and do some vibration of god names to make sure you are fully earthed and everything is finished.

Directional orientation

Ask yourself what is the largest flow of energy in your immediate vicinity? The ancient Egyptians had a clear answer to this, the river Nile. According to Margaret Murray, this accounts for the precise compass orientation of the pyramids of Giza, as the Nile flows precisely north south at that point. There is an interesting principle here that can be applied in any locale. At Abydos the direction of the Nile indicates what is called local north, (it differs from magnetic north by several degrees.) The whole temple is orientated to local north.

.....

The courts are connected with the following mysteries -

The mysteries of material success, which was represented by Ramesses I (Seti's son) as his military victories. Bear in mind that the Egyptians recognised no radical distinction between religious and military purposes.

The mysteries of earthly love including family and friendship.

The mysteries of water and especially the sacred river as the nurturing source of all life. These were depicted as androgynous river gods, one for each of the *nomes,* as they termed the adminstrative provinces of Ancient Egypt.

The mysteries of divine religion in its exoteric form - i.e. as official religion and its relationship to the ruler and the ordinary people.

Bibliography

Omm Sety (Dorothy Eady) and Hanny El Zeini, *Abydos: Holy City of Ancient Egypt*,LL Company, 1981.

Omm Sety, *Omm Sety's Abydos*, Benben Publications, Society for the Study of Egyptian Antiquities Studies [SSEA] No 3, Edited by Daniel M. Kolos. Canada? 1984

Lediard, ? The Life of Sethos translated from Greek into French.

Grafton-Milne J & Crum, WE, *The Osirion at Abydos*, with sections

Murray, Margaret, 'Astrological Character of Egypian Magical Wands' *in Proceeding of Society of Biblical Archeology*

Rosalie David A (Anne Rosalie), *A guide to religious ritual at Abydos*

Donadoni, *La decorazione della Tomba de Sethos I* [at valley of kings?)

Gardiner, A H, *Temple of Sethos I at Abydos*.

Colt, Jonathan, *The Search fo Omm Sety* (Rider)

Baldick, Julian Black God - *The Afroasiatic Roots of the Jewish, Christian and Muslim Religions*, IB Tauris 1996

Murray, Margaret, 'Tomb of the Two Brother' ??

Gaster, T H, *Thespis, ritual, myth and dram in the ancient near east*, Anchor 1961.

Notes

1   That the Osiris legend was known in many parts of the globe is investigated by Margaret Murray in an article 'The Cult of the drowned in Egypt' pamphlet 51 band 1913. Murray compares it with similar folklore in Europe and elsewhere eg: In a northern legend tells how three pious sisters were drowned when on a voyage together; their bodies were washed ashore on different parts of the coast of Denmark; each sister was canonised (the medieval form of deification) and a fountain sprang from her grave (Thorpe, Northern Mythology II, p. 217).Murray also quotes the *Heimskringla* of Snorri Sturlinson, where a Norwegian king Halfdan the black, a descendent of ...frey, was drowned at the age of forty by breaking off the ice in the spring. His body was recovered and divided into pieces; the fragments being buried in different parts of his kingdom to ensure fertility. The epithet 'the black' is same as applied to Osiris, Kem-ur 'the great black one.'

2   Murray obviously didn't know about the Sati legend, else she would have quoted it. Her sole Hindu citations are of a legend from Khotan in Kashgar, wher Mieou went into the river as a sacrifice to the river goddess and became a god (Hartland, *Legend of Perseus* III, 73, 74) and the rain making rocks or 'shalgramma' said to be a form of Vishnu, see Ward, *A View of the Hindoos* II pp. 222, 223.

3   Siegfried Schott *Bemerkungen zum ägyptischen Pyramidenkott (Berträge zur ägyptishchen Bauforschung und Alttertomsckunde Vol 5)* Cairo 1950. Quoted in I E S Edwards *The Pyramids of Egypt* (Pelican 1947/1970)

4 Sexual Magick

'The mind cannot be fully awake without the assistance of the body'

Attitudes to the body is probably the issue that most divides the magi from that of other religious practitioners. It is often possible through debate to reach some kind of common ground, even with Christians, on the nature of humanity's religious quest and the place of magick in that quest. But there is always an irreducible issue that comes between us. That issue is the role of the body and more especially sexuality in that quest. To put it bluntly, most of the religions of the west have a horror of the flesh. Magicians could perhaps have guaranteed themselves a quiet life if they had adopted the prevailing puritan values. It is not so unlikely, as I argue in my book *Sexual Magick*, the ancient pagan world had plenty of examples of puritanism - for example the Stoics who taught control of feelings and passions. Be that as it may, in the modern reemergence of magick, puritanism has played a very minor role. There is a vain hope that calling ourselves a fertility cult might win over some of our critics. But it seems doubtful if fertility was ever really an important part of the magical tradition. Our ancient Stone Age ancestors may well have had quite a jaudiced view of fertility. Fertility = more mouths to feed = hardship. The ancient Egyptian cultures practiced widespread contraception and the methods used are almost always recorded in magical texts. Magick is an ecstatic cult whose members are into sex not fertility.

I suppose there is a naive belief amongst sexual magicians that the penis is a magical wand and that the vagina is the magical cross or rood, which is conjured by it. For example Crowley's ritual *The Star Sapphire* begins

> *'Let the Adept be armed with his Magick Rood (and provided with his Mystic Rose).'*

Symonds and Grant, the editors of the above text, say in a footnote that the 'Magick Rood is the rod or wand of the Magician, in this context the erect penis. The 'Mystic Rose' is the Holy Grail or Cup of the Priestess, i.e. her vagina.'[1] Temperamentally I feel the need to get away from this kind of one-dimensional symbolism. In tantrism there is a concept known as the body yantra. This symbol has many complex levels of symbolism - but I think that at least one of these is that the whole body can be viewed as a wand. If you accept this view then you've de-centred the genitals and the crude facts of gender and entered a polymorphous world where all can interact on a much more equal basis. It doesn't matter what you've got, male or female, large or small - we've all got a body, we've all got a magick wand, should you choose to use it.

Sexual Magick ought to be really simple. Aleister Crowley, an early twentieth century advocate of its use, said it was a much *simpler* way to achieve the various aims of magick than the traditional complexity of the Golden Dawn Hermetic system. It was only simple because Crowley was completely permeated by the cosmology and precepts of his early training. It is like this, when I was younger, I used to listen to the radio a lot, especially *Luxemburg* which at the time was the only channel that played the kind of music I liked. I'd sit around with my friends listened to scratchy little renditions of progressive rock on a tiny transistor radio. It worked for us because we already knew the tune, or at least the way it should kind of go. We were so permeated by the rock and roll of the times, that the merest hint of the musick was enough to evoke in our minds the full technicolor version. If our parents heard the same sounds, they would probably wonder what all the fuss was about. Sexual magick is perhaps like that, the mind is charged with magick by our study and ritual training. Add to this the powerful opening up of the psyche that can be brought about by good lovemaking and you have the formula for a real trip into hyper reality. As Bhima, a character in the *Mahabharata,* put it so succinctly:

'Love, well made can lead to liberation.'

I suppose what I'm saying is that you need to prime the brain with something before the 'simple' techniques of magick can really work - in other words, it's not that simple! I guess we all sooner or later meet members of that caste of know-it-alls, who seem to have done everything and ought by all accounts to be some kind of enlightened master or demi-god. Mention *kundalini* in this company and you're sure to have someone there who will have raised his fire snake up and down his or her spine several times a day and can open and close their multiple chakras at the drop of a hat. I wouldn't dream of pricking their bubble but can't help asking myself what good has it done them? They often lack the experience and breadth of knowledge to really make much of it. There's a rumour that in the higher degrees of the OTO, the 'adept' must construct for themselves a special Masonic square, which they use to measure the degree made of their penises immediately following intercourse. An adept is issued with a secret grimoire that correlates this angle with a list of possible spheres on the tree of life. It is true honest, I read it somewhere.

Talking about your sexual (and indeed magical) experience can be very exposing. I often think that my own experience of sexuality is probably so perverse it couldn't really be of much relevance to anyone else. But I discovered that most sensitive people feel the same way and that the reason you share sexual experience is not as an exercise in oneupmanship, but rather to add another piece in the puzzle. It was very liberating for me to discover that everyone's experience of sex is as different as my own. Do you remember before you ever really had sex, how you'd hang on the words of the older boys (or girls) and repeat them to your own friends as if they were your own experiences? Many people internalize this and actually begin experiencing real sex with the model they have gleaned from countless locker room exchanges.

'What were you doing last night?'

'I was on the nest with some slag.'

'What does a woman want'

'a big cock'

'If your cocks as big as your mouth I'll take you home with me'

'I hate gentle sex'

'Is there anyone in here with me?'

'fuck me, fuck me now'

'Think of anything but what you're doing then you won't come too quick'

'The bigger the cushion the better the pushing'

Etc

In my book on sexual magick I make a start at exploring the ideas of post orgasmic states. It took me a while to come round to this point of view because I gotten the idea somewhere that sexual magick invariably involved avoidance of orgasm and some kind of trancey pre-orgasmic state. I really value the orgasm and wanted to enjoy it and let go of the feelings of guilt that can sometimes go with that. Sensitive people tie themselves in knots over this issue - allowing yourself to be pleasured by your partner - to give in to sensation and not feel that you are primarily there to pleasure your partner and not the other way round. Men can be especially sensitive to this, unless you are the typical lager drinking quick squirter, one of those 'sharrons or trevors' (with apologies to

Sharron and Trevor) who haunt tense nightclubs run by the Rank corporation. I once knew of a Trevor who damaged his sciatic nerve playing rugby. After that he could pump away all night if need be. What an animal, he could keep it up all night. Problem was that he could never come and this made 'Sharron' very miserable. She'd go to nightclubs with her friends just to find a *selfish* man - a quick shag on someone's mac in the mall car park might not sound very satisfying, but as she said, at least he came.

I once had a partner who read women's magazines all the time. I learnt a lot by reading the copies she left on the bathroom floor. My eye was caught by an article entitled 'Outercourse'. Full sexual intercourse generates some kind of bonding spark between the partners. Continuous exchange of this 'spark' can in some ways signal the end of ecstatic sex and a move towards something more enduring. Perhaps you don't want that? Why not avoid intercourse, perhaps altogether and try outercourse instead. I float the suggestion that sexual magick in a group should definitely be more outercourse than intercourse. Intercourse is a terminal event - on the whole it is a pleasure for two people and if you start with more than two, unless you are very skillful, the extras are likely to end up holding their own.

If you excluded this possibility altogether from the ritual, then the wide zone of outercourse could continue indefinitely and without the damage. The Sex Maniacs Ball and other encounter clubs can be like that. *Cosmopolitan* calls it Outercourse, Tuppy Owens prefers flirting. The rule of these events is that anything short of full intercourse (which would be illegal in a public place anyway) can occur. There are always a few sex starved who are desperate, but most are happy to let the unresolved sexual frisson create a divine atmosphere and tension. This could apply to an act of collective magick. All the participants need to have some level of attraction for each other. No one can turn off the little green eyed monster of jealously completely. In a group ritual, being naked together may be as far as the group wants to go, but even this is usually enough to generate the necessary magical tension to do the business.

A more common arena for sexual magick is still the one on one. The tension and affinity may have been building for a long time, weeks perhaps even years. Perhaps it is a one-night stand or a secret admiration, attraction or crush. Yes, you could throw up everything and run off and get married but you might find that the energy isn't there anymore. It is replaced by a different, perhaps just as important connection. Some people find the tension engendered in the early part of a relationship quite enervating - they can't eat properly or think straight. Others thrive on this tension. If you are in the latter group and find your creativity growing in leaps and bounds then you might like to extend this by avoiding full sexual intercourse. These days of safe sex have done a lot to extend this domain. No longer does a man need to bury his penis in the vagina. You can after all do anything short of sexual intercourse - stroking, touching, kissing, massage, mutual masturbation, sucking, licking, finger fucking (I'm sure you can think of loads more than I can).

Without full sexual intercourse the energy is, in my opinion, never completely earthed and the ritual never terminated. You may 'come forth' several times but it is still not complete, that terminating spark has not been exchanged enough times for you to lose interest. Your body can end up shaking with lust. I would at this point refer you to a book by Jan Fries entitled *Seidways - shaking, swaying and serpent mysteries* and remind you that spontaneous shaking can lead to magical trance.

I approach this kind of thing in a magical state. I like to revert to the playful and polymorphous sexuality of my childhood. I hate it when people get too serious about sex. Some partners are so serious about the whole thing. They need to learn to play again. Play is a very undervalued aspect of human consciousness. For some sex is supposed to be a serious thing not a game, where you can stop half way and discuss a change in the rules.

'Do you like to have your nipples sucked... shall I do it harder?'

In childish sex play, you don't need any concept of the whole thing, where it is going. Maybe it stops here; I need no overall view of whether I can stay the course to the end. Performance does not matter, merely the moment, as long as your are enjoying that. The serious minded sex magician might think, can I do the great rite? If I am a man, I might think to myself, will I be able to get it up, is my prick big enough to make my partner come forth. You're already focused on the end. What does the women think, is my cunt too big, are my tits big enough will I be wet enough, do I make the right noises when I come, should I say something spooky ?' Could it also be that the outercourse body is more versatile?

Magick in groups may need some conventions but one on one you can do what the hell you like. I really like the sexual magical experiments of Yeats and his wife George. They contacted their spirit guides and just spoke to each other without all the usual trappings and conventions of the spiritualist séance palour. It was very liberating sex magical play and the results were really amazing (see later chapter).

In the occult tradition there is a whole system of sexual magick that divides the mystery into a number of degrees based on whether the activity is autoerotic, with a heterosexual or a homosexual partner. I said in my book *Sexual Magick* that this kind of distinction didn't make a lot of sense to me. Maybe what I've written so far helps to explain why. When you exclude terminal intercourse, what's left is a large gray area of sexual connection that is common ground between all sexes and genders and this is where, in my opinion, the most fertile area for sexual magick exists.

I suggested in *Sexual Magick*, that the process of magical exploration of your body yantra should perhaps begin alone. As the mythographer Joseph Campbell says - the magical life journey is something that may have companions along the way but which you finish by yourself. You enter your temple naked. Learn to enjoy this, to feel the air on your skin and the glow of freedom. Naked bodies smell different, smell yourself and learn to love yourself, every part. I tried to express this with a poem called *Ode to the Cock and Fanny.*

Ode to the Cock and Fanny
[with apologies ot EE Cummins]

I really like my cock
I like what it does
I like the way that each day it surprises me with its moods
Sometimes calm and thoughtful
other swollen, straining against my trousers.
At a word you're ready for anything
In the presence of the yoni
you are always willing to offer your all
You are a religious icon
worshipped in thousands of temples throughout the world.
To see you gives me good luck
You always comfort me
if I am alone
I like to stroke you
until the clear elixir begins to flow
and I can run my fingers easily
over your head and neat shaft.
If in the past I ever expressed regret
at your shape or dimension
I take it all back now
you are in every way perfect.
You give me such pleasure
willingly and unreservedly
I love the feel of you
and the way you fit so neatly in my

lover's organ
Stay with me always
lead me into the ways of pleasure
for thine is the comedom
the stimulator and the messy one
for ever and ever
a man

The yoni replies
I really like my fanny
I like what it does
I like the way that each day it surprises me with its moods
Sometimes calm and thoughtful
other hot and wet dying to be touched.
Sometimes a mere word gets me going
or the sight and feel of a hard cock
sliding near my legs, touching my clitoris with its wet tip
All offerings are acceptable to me, large or small
I am also a religious icon
worshipped everywhere
To see me dispels all evil influences
When you stroke me with a finger or tongue
I quiver with excitement
Soon the clear love juice flows
from me, from my lover, mouth and cock
Mouth, nipples and clitoris, these three are apiece
I love the feel of you, finger inside, tongue in me.

If when bloodied and bowed I think on you

you are in every way perfect.

Thrust hard into me, or let me gentle slide over your cock

I don't mind, I love it all ways

Stay in me

and I will lead you in the ways of pleasure

with or without a condom

for ever and ever

yes

Once a long time ago I went out into my beloved sacred landscape. It was night and I was alone. I looked up into the clear heavens and drew down the power of one of the constellations. I was depressed because a relationship had just come to a sticky end. The element of earth is not the planet earth; it is the entire ground of being. The northern quantrant of the circle is said to correspond to the element earth, and the 'ultimate' point of north is the sky itself and the stars and dark matter it contains. This is another sacred landscape.

Much later, a person came and we became close. We made a temple and as two divine beings played together as we wilt. One morning, not too long after that, I awoke and that person had gone. I never saw them again. Recently I managed to reconnect with that experience and earth it here in the form of a poem. I'd always liked the work of the mystical Bengali poet Tagore and the ancient bards of India, who really encapsulated for me the erotic and magical sentiment. I really love Tagore's version of an ancient tantrik theme - the *Cloud Messenger*. Tagore's version is divine but I wanted to try in my own feeble way to rewrite it so it meant something for me. It was a long ambition and reconnecting with my own demon lover I did it. For what its worth here goes:

Cloud Messenger
Are there clouds where you are?
There are clouds here now, many clouds
Perhaps as the winds change
They will move to the east
And by some obscure and tortuous route
These same clouds will pass over your head
Such was the thought of the ancient poet
Precipitating the misery of all separated lovers

Perhaps those same trade winds
That brought your ancestors
Will draw my cloud messenger
Down, down toward the hot equator
Where men, fearing the power of women
Cover them
As the cool evening comes, I look down
On secret meetings, where, hair loosed
Women sweat, and convulsing their bodies
Call demon lovers
Their great black tresses hang down,
I blow them a kiss and reveal myself

148 Tankhem

For an instance, a patch of moist emotion,
In their dryness

Now a long journey
Over nameless oceans
Where old ones rule
Guided by instinct
Darkness below me,
Unfamiliar stars above me
I am a feint trace of consciousness
Trying to touch something
In all this darkness
Call me
And guide me in
Let me come
Lying over you
Your body strong beneath me
Like the earth
Reveal yourself
To a gentle breeze
That blows from me
Caressing your skin
Open, as I open before you
And cooling drops of rain
Will fall upon you.

The Erotic Landscape revisited

'Divided for Love's Sake - For the Chance of Union'

I was first introduced to the connection between eroticism and the sacred landscape many years ago, during the course of a short but intense relationship with a well-known visionary artist, who, for the sake of this article, I will call Dakini Devi. My first attempt to record some of these experiences formed the basis of the chapter 'The Erotic Landscape' that appeared in my book *Sexual Magick*.[2] This chapter discussed the way in which certain magical trance states help the magician develop a connection between their inner world and the physical landscape that surrounds them. Through sexuality the magician develops a special gaze in which he or she is able to see places of power in the landscape. As my senses became more tuned in and I could see the remains of sacred landscapes and even create new ones - I remember Dakini saying to me one day, that I was beginning to develop the gaze. It is almost as if you begin to see the sensual flesh of the land - as for example at the 'manger' below Uffington White Horse in Berkshire. The technique in itself is stupidly simple, merely go to a sacred site, stay there for a while, get to know it, mellow out, sleep etc etc. This way the landscape becomes embedded in your brain; it begins to live there. At peak moments, such as during lovemaking, the landscape may choose to come to life, either in your head, your partner's head or sometimes both at once.

Together we went to the ancient stone-age ritual complex at Avebury in Wiltshire. Dakini, who knew almost everything there was to know about this place, initiated me into its mysteries. It is a place that has been close to my heart ever since. Dakini taught me how to connect with the nameless divine beings of the site, these forces would later erupt into our consciousness, as we made love within the sacred space of our temple room. Intuitively it seemed that the Avebury ritual site had an erotic component and this seemed yet another example of the mindset found also in Tantrism and in even in the more earthy, shamanic byways of Egyptian magick. These ideas took root and as I moved towards the task of creating my own magical system or synthesis, these experiences formed part of the process. This system I call Tankhem - which traces the Tantrik doctrines of the Hindu intellectual tradition back to their Egyptian origins and forms a bridge to the nameless or primeval beings of the predynastic and Neolithic times.

I'm often asked, why this obsession with ancient philosophy? I suppose the attraction of ancient thought is that by some strange twist of fate, ancient ideas often become modern ones. As we as a species develop and grow, we are able again to understand the thoughts of our ancestors. This is a fairly familiar idea in academic philosophy as the following example might help to illustrate. The pagan philosopher Plato continues to dominate the modern mind. Plato developed the techniques of Greek drama into a powerful way of exteriorizing ideas through the use of dialogue. He wrote dialogues in which important mystical themes were played out. However some of these dialogues have only really been fully understood within the last one hundred years, when our own minds had began to move in a similar direction. There are long passages in Plato dealing with the nature of the body and what makes it sick or healthy, which have been largely ignored until in recent years we, as a culture, have began looking for alternatives to the modern clinical model. Our understanding of the ancient mind is something that can only come about when our own minds begin to tread the same pathways, to speak the same dialogues.

Egyptian magick attracted me because it is so old yet so subtle. Since the closure of all pagan temples by the Christian despot Theodosius, its secrets became really secret, even the language of the writing was forgotten and its magical landscapes and temples buried beneath the surface of the desert. As the lights on the sanctuary were extinguished, the doctrine of the magi survived outside of the Christian sphere of influence in practices such as Tantrism. Even the driest academic book acknowledges this fact, and I give several examples of this in my own book. Tantrism, is one of the most liberating of ancient ideas, if ancient thoughts were all like Tantrism then we would have to say that the ancients definitely knew something they we moderns do not, and that they knew things that we desperately need to relearn. Primarily the sacred and mystical nature of our own bodies and the wonderful capacity of the sexual act to change the structures of our brain as it did for our ancient ancestors - the first Tantriks.

When it comes to understanding the magick of 'preliterate' times before the coming of the dynasties, the task seems hopeless; the gods of places such as Avebury seem destined to remain forever veiled. Some might say that we can never really know how the ancient magicians thought or did things - but I do not share this pessimism. Magick and ritual has its own archaeology, if there is space in a stone circle or temple to move around and dance, it may well be that our ancestors used it in such a way. The site 'teaches' us how it can or could be used, we try out these techniques and learn even more about the site. Eventually we are perhaps acting as the ancient masters did, and there is a saying, if you repeat the actions of the master, then you become the master. Perhaps as we use the ancient techniques of the magi, we can become them and they will begin to speak to us over the long intervening silence?

Over the last few years, I began researching further into the nature of the temple. A magical temple can, in itself, be viewed as an idealized sacred landscape. Temples are also stylized representation of the human body - (see *Sexual Magick*). I feel that the idea of the temple is so familiar that we are in danger of overlooking its mystery, the creation of sacred space. In the texts that have survived from ancient Egypt, it is possible to perceive the archaeology of gnosis - the texts contain many layers of meaning - nothing seems to be wasted. In other words, you have to mentally move around and inhabit the temple using visioning techniques, in order to really learn what the landscape is trying to teach you. Even though these insights, for what they are worth, are inspired by my magical work with the Tankhem system, I know that some might find it easier to accept, if they had some independent corroboration. Intuitively I felt that the position of a sacred text in the temple, whether it be in the outer court or in the inner sanctuary, would somehow, be relevant to its meaning. And I discovered that the German archaeologist Siegfried Schott had indeed advanced a similar theory in the 1950s.

The earliest temples and sacred landscapes have hardly survived. The Pyramid Texts, so called because they were carved on the walls of the pyramids of the 5th and 6th dynasty Kings, (c. 2500BC), record spells such as 'The bricks are removed for thee from the great tomb'.[3] This text is carved on a stone building but talks of brick - the scribe is quoting from an even older text, when sacred architecture was made of brick - it is quoting from 'books' even older than the time of the Pyramids! The earlier sacred buildings were of brick and before that they were of natural organic materials such as wood and reed, with perhaps the occasional use of megalithic stones, as the following article in a recent addition of *Nature* indicates:

Megaliths and Neolithic astronomy in southern Egypt

The Sahara west of the Nile in southern Egypt was hyperarid and unoccupied during most of the Late Pleistocene epoch. About 11,000 years ago the summer monsoons of central Africa moved into Egypt, and temporary lakes or playas were formed. The Nabta playa depression, which is one of the largest in southern Egypt, is a kidney-shaped basin of roughly 10km by 7km in area. The authors report the discovery of megalithic alignments and stone circles next to locations of Middle and Late Neolithic communities at Nabta, which suggests the early development of a complex society.

The southward shift of the monsoons in the Late Neolithic age rendered the area once again hyperarid and uninhabitable some 4,800 radiocarbon years before the present (years BP). This well-determined date establishes that the ceremonial complex of Nabta, which has alignments to cardinal and solstitial directions, was a very early megalithic expression of ideology and astronomy. Five megalithic alignments within the playa deposits radiate outwards from megalithic structures, which may have been funerary structures. The organization of the megaliths suggests a symbolic geometry that integrated death, water, and the Sun. An exodus rom the Nubian Desert at ~4,800 years B[efore] P[resentday] may have stimulated social differentiation and cultural complexity in predynastic Upper Egypt.

J M Malville, F Wendorf, A A Mazar & R Schild
Megaliths and Neolithic astronomy in southern Egypt
(Letters to *Nature*)
Nature 392, 488 (1998)

Other texts describe these very first sacred landscapes, describing buildings that, even for the ancient Egyptians, were a fading and distant memory. The earliest mythologies often talk of the first or primal building. They did not even know the names of the gods that roamed during those days of yore but referred to them cryptically in books such as the 'Book of the Primeval Old Ones' as the nameless gods.

The non magician tends to focus overly on the surface exterior form of ceremony and ritual, whilst having very little understanding of the inner states implied by these techniques. I like to interpret them using a psychological model. 'The Book of the Primeval Old

Ones' (a pukka book not a Grantian creation)[4] tells that in the primeval times, the surface of the planet was covered with water. Below the water lay the remains of one or perhaps more than one previous creation. The divine entities were without form but not without power. The ancient sages or shamans, call out to these beings, using words of power that they had but recently learnt. There are said to be seven sages or shamans and this is a motif that seems to crop up all over the place. I have found references to them in Egyptian, Hindu and even Chinese mythology, where they are connected with the constellation the Plough or Great Bear. Apart from an astrological significance, they seem to me to be real personality types, perhaps members of the tribe whose trance awareness is slightly more advanced than the others and are thus able to say, 'that is a special place, we should build a temple here'.

At the word of the seven shamans the power quickened and the first cosmic island rose from the waters. On this island, those shamans or seers built the first sacred temple. Perhaps it was these visionaries whose consciousness first emerged randomly from the past. (Interestingly, it was another visionary, Imhotep, who was later to be credited with the creation of the first temple hewn from stone, and was subsequently deified for his efforts.) These are very suggestive images - I feel they have something to do with the moment in which our early predator mentality emerged from its instinctual fog and became self aware. The divine forces take on form where previously they had none - they are still nameless but now they are represented in two of the most ancient hieroglyphs - the hand and the yoni or phallus (see Lascaux). These 'hieroglyphs' are very ancient indeed, perhaps even the oldest representations of the divine. These same pictograms can be seen in the cave paintings of the Paleolithic - for example at Pech Merle, Lot, France (c. 24,000BCE), where the scribe has left the imprint of his or her own hand on the sacred 'pictographic' text. The cave paintings are revealed, not as pictures in the sense of art history, but as sacred texts - whose true meaning is only now emerging. My editor reminds me that magick is full of trance meditations using the human hand as a focus; see Jan Fries *Seidways*[5] for an interesting exploration of some of these wyrd byways of magick.

What do these two pictograms mean - the hand and the phallus? Psychologically I feel they are pointing to the catalyst that enabled our consciousness to mutate and become self-aware. Is it not obvious that what most distinguishes us from other beasts of creation is our sexuality - what other animal has a sexuality quite like ours? We look at other animals and try to recognize a rudimentary sexuality e.g. love-play in dolphins and non-reproductive homosexuality in various other animals? Perhaps some animals are closer to our end of the sexual spectrum than others but I still feel that strictly speaking, animals reproduce they do not have sex. The ancient Egyptians seem to be telling us that it was in the sexual act itself that the ancients first found the way to become human. It was sexuality that generated the power necessary to raise the primal mound from the waters, where it had subsided after some primeval battle. Why should this have been a once and for all time process? Could not the same catalyst work over and over again? Two principles become divided from each other in order to become self-aware and then experience the real transforming joy of union.

The two gods - hand and genitals - are later assimilated into the predynastic cult of the phallic god Min[6] and his 'cousin' Amon-Ra - whose rites in dynastic times included some form of sexual magick - in which the phallus of the god was stimulated and a magical, transformative elixir sprang forth. The mythology of dynastic times fully explores all the mysteries of sacred sexuality starting with masturbation. A mythology that gives such a central role to an act of masturbation is a very mysterious one. Perhaps they knew something we do not or have forgotten. They seem to be saying that masturbation is good for the body, good for the land and good for the whole topocosm. It is also one of the first mysteries of life, when we first reach out and touch ourselves. On the face of it touching ourselves seems unnecessary, for we are already touching 'inside'. Somehow the system by some accident of physiology, finds this one of the first magical arts - perhaps this is why the later religions sought to suppress and demonize the process? We most of us have residual conditioning concerning masturbation - but the ancients knew, as we now know, that masturbation is a natural part of the healthy functioning of mind, body, spirit - the works. Paradoxically, the way you learn and practice masturbation affects your ability to really experience sacred sex with another person. Look how many of the current problems of dysfunctional sex stem from ineffective masturbation. For example for men, the problem can be an addiction to furtive and rapid relief, whilst for women it is an ignorance due to lack of exploration and experimentation with self love.

Beginning with masturbation, or self love, and embracing the range of joyous sexuality, the magician can reprogramme, his or her whole biosystem so that it become fully in tune with the erotic landscape. It is said that we contain the whole of our evolution in our genes - that when a human develops from embryo to adult, they go through all the phases of millions of years of evolution, from fish to reptile to mammal. If this be true for the physical, may it not also be true for consciousness itself? The writer Gyrus says that this reprogramming involves retracing the development of consciousness, union to division to union etc., back again and I agree with that. For men and women the first step might be work on developing your orgasm, so that it become a total body experience that literally 'fucks your brains out', a useful condition to be in, when exploring some of the better trance states. I am particularly fond of Margot Anand's book *Art of Sexual Magick*,[7] where she gives graded exercises for exploring your orgasmic response. This can be done alone or with a trusted partner. Even if your sexual partner is present, the ideal is still to explore your *individual* sexual response first, the partner helping to stimulate and explore the secret workings of your body at your pleasure. The idea is to enter your ritual space without any particular goal in mind, just enjoy the full bodily sensations as he or she caresses and strokes your body. Being pleasured by your partner is in many ways more intimate that actual intercourse. Don't worry about coming forth, just become very pacific and let the sensations stream around your body. Your partner will naturally vary the rhythm making the approach to climax slower and more erratic. If you feel yourself approaching the point of 'no return', maybe ask your partner to pause, and make any adjustments necessary to prevent ejaculation or climax (for a man, pressing on the prostate or muladhara chakra can often help this - or as Norman Mailer writes in his highly charged novel *Ancient Evenings*,[8] 'to bank up the fire of the testicles').

As the urge for ejaculation or release subsides, you may feel the warm sexual glow spreading throughout your whole pelvic region, opening out other energy centres sometimes called chakras. When you're ready your partner begins again, exploring all your erogenous zones or places of power, until you reach another peak. The first time you try this exercise, you might be happier coming off now, but if you are more experienced, you might want to go for another and another pre-orgasmic peak. A strange thing happens, you become like an erotic landscape, a sea of sensation. Try to regard the time you have spent in this 'build up' to ejaculation, as part of the orgasm. Viewed this way, perhaps you can see that an orgasm, for both men and women, is actually a lot more intense than those few moments of ejaculation. Perhaps you are happy to just stop when you've had enough, although you might find that when you do come in the conventional sense, the orgasm is ultra physical and polymorphous. In others it forms a field all over your body. There are at least two distinct sexual trance states here, one 'pre-orgasmic' the other 'post orgasmic'. Both can be moments in which ancestral memories, dreams, meditations and archaic god forms can break through into your sensitized body. That is sexual magick.

Locked away in our brains, are the first moments during which we emerged as humans from the cosmic waters, becoming self aware and preserving that moment in the form of sacred landscapes - temples, reed enclosures and circles? Perhaps you will remember that first moment when, as ancient hunter-gatherer, you made love or stimulated your partner and something in the way you thought about the world around you changed utterly. Maybe you were that naked man in a cave at Lascaux, staring at the bison and rhinoceros and as you look down you see your erection. Later you paint your experience on the walls of the cave.[9] The Tankhem magical system works like this - combining a primeval sexuality with a re-membering of the first temple - that we can live again as our ancestors did - in other words - we can turn our brains back on. One hint as to the accomplishment of this task lies in the understanding and reclaiming of our sexuality and the connections it has always had to the external and erotic landscape.

Notes

1   *Liber ABA, Magick,* edited by J Symonds and K Grant (RKP 1973.) There is a new edition out from Weisers, edited by the head of a rival magical order. Although this casts some doubt on some of Symonds and Grant's other annotations, it is silent on this. ′

2.   This remaining section first appeared as an article in *Towards 2020 magazine,* IV, 1998. *Sexual Magick* was actually written under the name Katon Shual, published by Mandrake of Oxford in 1988 reprinted in 1995.

3   Quoted in *The Pyramids of Egypt* by I E S Edwards (Pelican 1947). Spell 355 p. 193).

4.   *The Mythological Origin of the Egyptian Temple* E A E Reymond, Manchester University Press 1969

5   Jan Fries, *Seidways - shaking swaying and serpent mysteries* (Mandrake of Oxford 1997)

6   Predynastic means in this context the 1000 years or so before the first dynastic king, circa 3000BC. The Min statue found at Koptos and now in the Ashmolean Museum, is perhaps one of the oldest pieces of stone sculpture to have survived from the ancient world.

7.   Margot Anand, *The Art of Sexual Magick,* Misses a lot of more esoteric stuff out but is basically a very sound book and a good basis for a discussion or first experiments in sexual magick.

8   Norman Mailer, *Ancient Evenings,* (Picador 1984)

9   J.D. Lewis-Williams' book *Believing and Seeing: Symbolic meanings*

in Southern San rock paintings.

5 Twenty Eight

Yeats the Magician

In 1995 I went on holiday to Ireland. On a day too wet to explore the limestone pavements of the Burren I made my way over to Gort, looking for the lair of the poet WB Yeats and his lifelong friend and patron Lady Gregory. In an act of municipal vandalism, the remains of Coole Park, the Gregory countryseat, were pulled down in the 1960s. I suspect that following the 1921 partition of Ireland, it suffered the fate of many an Anglo Irish household and was burnt out. So the place that inspired so many magical poems is no more, although it is still possible to wander in the park, now open to the public and meditate upon those magical swans:

Unwearied still, lover by lover,
They paddle in the cold
Companionable streams or climb the air;

Their hearts have not grown old;

Passion or conquest, wander where they will,

Attend upon them still.

(from The Wild Swans At Coole 1919)

When in Ireland, Yeats wanted to live close to his friend Lady Gregory and he bought a ruined Norman tower house called Ballylee Castle or Thoor Ballylee and began renovation. Ireland is dotted with these gloomy monuments, built by the invading Normans to protect their new conquest from the remains of the Celtic aristocracy. The Norman invasion of Ireland really does represent the end of the Celtic world and the substitution of a more patrician Christian church for the plebeian Celtic variety. The Tower house is now one of several museums dedicated to the life and poetry of Yeats - perhaps Ireland's greatest twentieth century poet. Yeats was never able to completely fulfill his plan to make this tower his permanent base. His growing involvement in Irish politics and then ill heath necessitated another warmer home. Even so magical events occurred here, and the curators of the museum have captured this in the museum's design.

The Yeatses bought the tower in 1915 but it was pretty much uninhabitable until 1918. After a magical journey through Galway and the west of Ireland, the Yeatses made a point of finishing off their odyssey with a session at the tower on the equinox, i.e. c 21 September 1918. This was to be the first of many magical rituals performed in the tower, either in its rooms or occasionally, so it is said, on the roof. The roof is a particularly good place for elemental rituals; high above the surrounding trees and open to the bleak Atlantic gales that thrust their way across the plain. Their first session had to be brief because, as they wrote in their magical diary, the place was still 'very cold'.

It is interesting to see how much Aleister Crowley followed Yeats's activities, making a point of including the Tower house as a setting for an important incident in his novel *Moonchild*, written in 1917, i.e. two years after the Yeatses' purchase of the place. A character in Crowley's novel called 'Gates' is magically attacked at the tower and falls to his death. The story's narrator tells us that Gates 'had been to the church in the village near Posilippo, whose tower overlooked the 'butterfly-net'; and he had persuaded the priest to allow him continual access to that tower, on the pretext of being an artist. And indeed he had a *pretty amateur talent for painting in water-colours.*' (p. 161 Weiser Edition, my emphasis). The 'butterfly net', is a code name used by the characters in the novel for the magical operation of creating a moonchild. That is a complex operation of sexual magick in which the participants conceive a child and then attempt to persuade a spirit of a higher spiritual entity to reincarnate into the developing foetus. Occult theory specified that the most appropriate time for such an operation be during the third month of foetal development when consciousness was said to begin in the womb. As we shall see, magical work such as this was not unknown in the Hermetic Order of the Golden Dawn, the source of Crowley's early training in magick.

Crowley had never physically visited the tower and made the incorrect assumption that the tower was a disused ecclesiastical building. Thus in *Moonchild*, a magical link is established between the XVI tarot trump, the blasted tower or church and Gates' hideaway bringing about its destruction by lightning.

There was obviously no love lost between Yeats and Crowley. In his publication *The Equinox*, Crowley, in a series of articles entitled 'My Crapulous Contemporaries', lampooned many of the occultists of his day, including W B Yeats. He crudely satirized Yeats's Celtic prose drama *The Shadowy Waters*, as the 'Shadowy Dill Waters', writing that 'It is true that a sort of dreary music runs monotonously through your verses, only jarred by the occasional discords. It is as if an eternal funeral passed along, and the motor-hearse had something wrong with the ignition and the exhaust.' (*Equinox* Vol II)

You might doubt Crowley's assessment of Yeats as an artist (and magician). But bear in mind that *The Shadowy Waters* was written in 1906, years before Yeats's great revelation. Indeed, Richard Ellmann, a modern scholar with a cooler head than Crowley's, seems to share some of his assessment - Ellmann says that 'had Yeats died instead of marrying in 1917, he would have been remembered as a remarkable minor poet who achieved a diction more powerful than that of his contemporaries but who, except in a handful of poems, did not have much to say with it.'[1]

The novel *Moonchild,* like a great deal of Crowley's writing, is strangely prophetic - especially in this instance of what was *about* to happen to Yeats in the *very* year of its publication. Yeats was indeed struck by a lightning bolt out of the blue. Those with literary ambitions take note, Yeats was born in 1865 and so was fifty two at the time, and the moral - it is never too late to start. It is also interesting in terms of magical development. Many of us learn magick over a much shorter time span that our predecessors of a few generations ago. Magical training and written material are now much more widely available. Even so, many of the more profound elements of the magical work require time and intellectual maturity if they are to really work. Yeats had been in the Hermetic Order of the Golden Dawn for the best part of twenty-eight years, by the time his real revelation and magical breakthrough came his way. He had done much important work in that organisation and before that in the Theosophical Society and diverse spiritualist groups. He waited a long time for the veil on the adytum to be lifted.

It is often assumed that Yeats's muse was Maud Gonne, the Irish nationalist and fellow member of Hermetic Order of the Golden Dawn. It is sometimes said that with her Yeats enjoyed what amounted to a spiritual marriage. This relationship became less important to him after his mundane marriage in 1917.

Relationships like Yeats and Maud Gonne can be likened to a variety of 'tantrism' called *sahajiyana* or the 'natural way'. Sahajiyans are often poets and artists who enter into secret and elicit trysts that fall outside of normal family or clan loyalties. These are what amount to largely unconsummated, unearthed love affairs. This has a very magical effect on the body which remains in a highly aroused state, often for many weeks, even years. By aroused, I do not necessarily mean the sexual centres, these may well be involved, but often the arousal is more noticeable in other parts of the 'psychological' anatomy. I still find the Tantrik chakra system the most convenient way to describe this - the arousal may be more noticeable in the stomach (manipura chakra), or 'heart' (anahata chakra), where it may be transferred to the throat or head chakras. This energy can be very tangible and it may be possible for it to physically flow between the corresponding chakras of the sahajiyan partners when they are in receptive mood. (See my book *Sexual Magick*, for some more information on this system.)

As there is often no satisfactory physical resolution of the passion, large amounts of psychic energy erupt into other areas, often as highly creative outbursts of poetry or art. Eventually the relationship burns itself out or the partners step over the line and the relationship falls apart. On the negative side, it seems that the pent up energy engendered by this magical practice can sometimes manifest as physical illness. Ancient medico-tantrik sources known as Ayurveda (the science of longevity), of which I am a student, say that Tuberculosis is the disease most often linked with the above psychic state and interestingly this disease is known across several cultures as a disease of lovers.

Yeats obviously felt a need to earth his highly creative magical partnership with Maud Gonne in the form of a full physical relationship, but this was not to be. Throughout their relationship Maud Gonne refused his every proposal of marriage dealing a final blow to Yeats's hopes when in 1903 she wrote to him from Paris that she had just married Major John McBride of the Irish Transvaal Brigade in the Boar War.

McBride was, according to Ellmann, not a poet, not an occultist, not a learned man and not even a good lover. It seemed a perverse choice of a husband. Predictably the effect on Yeats was devastating - it almost killed him. A London pathologist, and fellow member of the Hermetic Order of the Golden Dawn (Westcott,?) thought that he must have had tuberculosis. This was apparently confirmed by later X-ray, although luckily for Yeats the disease disappeared again. Serious as the disease was, and indeed still is, Yeats's experience of it shows that it is possible to escape its clutches. His recovery is not unusual given the help of friends and indeed the power of magick in its broadest sense.

Maud Gonne's husband John McBride was killed in the abortive Easter 1916 rising against the British colonial rule of Ireland.. This event was in itself something of a magical act. The participants knew beforehand that the action was doomed to failure, but went ahead because of the effect they thought it might (and in fact did) have on the popular imagination. So McBride turned out to be a magician after all and Yeats, although he hated McBride, saw that he had 'found [his] heroic opposite'[2] and Yeats, magnanimous to the last, immortalized him in the poem *Easter 1916*:

'This other man I had dreamed
A drunken, vainglorious lout,
He had done most bitter wrong
To some who are near my heart,
Yet I number him in the song;
He, too, has resigned his part
In the casual comedy;
He, too, has been changed in his turn,

Transformed utterly:

A terrible beauty is born.

The Hermetic roller coaster

Yeats's life began to pick up pace, and he entered a period that may be familiar to some modern occultists as the 'hermetic roller coaster'. Yeats rushed to Paris to again propose marriage to Maud Gonne on condition that she gave up politics. She refused. Despite this knock back, he stayed in Paris and struck up a friendship with Maud Gonne's daughter Iseult.

Iseult was Maud Gonne's daughter by a much earlier marriage. Iseult was born in 1894 in rather strange circumstances. When Yeats first met her mother Maud Gonne, she was, unbeknownst to him, already in love with a French newspaper editor by whom she had conceived a child. Sadly this child died. Yeats and his friend George Russell, author under the pseudonym AE of a mystical book entitled *The Candle of Vision*, was comforting Maud following this untimely death. She asked them what would happen to such a tiny soul. I think it was George Russell who pronounced that 'such souls were often reborn in the same family'.

Consumed by grief, Maud Gonne found the father and took him down to the burial vault in Sacré Cœur and made love to him over the dead child's coffin! Maud Gonne conceived and the child was called Iseult. The whole story is very reminiscent of Crowley's later novel *Moonchild*. It also has important parallels with the Hindu tantrik practice of savasadhana, or meditation on a corpse. Such rites are said to be still practiced in India, although they are very secret. An experienced tantrik magician and his assistant go to the cremation ground where fresh corpses are stored awaiting cremation the next day. Whilst the assistant keeps watch, the tantrik adept prepares a terrifying ritual in which a primordial goddess is invoked into the revivified corpse. The adept take a strong psychoactive potion and the rite can result in the most terrifying visions.

Maud Gonne's daughter Iseult, was in her early twenties at the time she was befriended by the much older Yeats. Inevitably he proposed to her, and after several months of presumable hard soul searching, she too turned him down.

Shortly after this final knock back, Yeats returned to England and took up with a woman friend called Georgie Hyde Lees, a woman he had known from his days in the Hermetic Order of the Golden Dawn. In October 1917, after a whirlwind romance, he married her. Now all the fun begins. As the proverb goes 'marry in haste, repent at leisure' and indeed Yeats did repent. For within a few days of their marriage he was having serious doubts about the wisdom of it all and sank into one of his deepest depressions. What a mistake he thought he had made.

Passive and active mediumship

The newlyweds were honeymooning in the Ashdown Forest in Sussex. Mrs Yeats, or 'George' as she was habitually called, seeing what a mood her husband was in thought she would do something to distract him. She was interested in psychic research and back in 1911 had helped Yeats to check the authenticity of information given him by mediums, so she knew a thing or two about parlour-room séances. As Ellmann puts it, 'she encouraged a pencil to write a sentence'[3] Here is what she wrote 'What you have done is right for both the cat and the hare.' She was the cat and the hare was Maud Gonne. The more cynically minded read into this that George was desperate to keep her unhappy husband and used a spiritualist trick to capture his attention and eventually his love. Whatever the truth, from these small, contrived beginnings, sprang what has been described as 'the most remarkable body of materials of its kind in the history of psychical research'.[4]

Over the course of the next three years, the couple recorded 3600 pages of automatic writing made during 450 sittings - by any standards a sizeable body of work. I wonder how many modern magicians can remember the last thirty rituals they were in, let along 400! And those 3600 pages of research are only that part of the communication that they choose to preserve. Much of it was lost, including the record of those first few crucial days. Even so, it makes Crowley/Aiwaz's *Book of the Law* look like a *billet doux*. Some of the communication was worked over by Yeats and published as a book entitled *A Vision*, which is as near as he ever got to constructing his own magical system.

The Yeatses training in the Golden Dawn would have instilled in them hostility toward common spiritualism. The Golden Dawn taught that passive mediumship was to be avoided at all costs. Passive mediumship is the kind of mediumship one can still see practiced in spiritualist churches. The medium enters a light trance and invites any spirits present to make use of him or her. The Golden Dawn taught that the medium should take a more active role, selecting and invoking appropriate spirits, which are then able to give a higher level of communication. This is not to deny remarkable results sometimes achieved by passive mediumship.[5] However many of the examples I and other investigators have witnessed, have been far from impressive and often faked.

In the Yeatses' experiments, they trod a middle path between passive and active mediumship. They often discarded large chunks of the script after later examination and checking. In fact it seems that William Yeats, was on the lookout for dodgy communications and later asked his wife for a list of the books in her library. He read every one of these books, to see if any of the more complex ideas might be derived from them - a suspicion that turned out to be quite unfounded.

What was the purpose of the communication?

Yeats was, to use a modern idiom, 'knocked out' by the content of the 'almost illegible script'. He found it so exciting and profound that he 'offered to spend the rest of his life explaining and piecing together those scattered fragments.'

> 'No' said the communicators firmly, 'we have come to give you *metaphors* for poetry'

And indeed, this is what happened.

William Yeats thereafter came 'to be ranked as the dominant poet of our time...largely responsible for founding a literary movement and for bringing a national theatre into being; he drew into creative energy Synge and Lady Gregory, strongly influenced a number of other writers and evolved a new way of writing verse.'[6] So very different to what Crowley called a *pretty amateur talent.* The communicators were true to their words and much more besides. It is also worth bearing in mind that poetry was in times past and certainly up until the time of Yeats, seen as a magical art form. In the Celtic world, it is well known that the Bards were expected to be proficient in poetry as a sign of their adeptship. So perhaps it was for William Yeats after he received the initiation of the bridal chamber and what he called the *Gift of Harun Al Rashid.*

The method

We can learn a lot from this. The communicators insisted that there were no observers. They dispensed with the normal paraphernalia of spiritualist trance. There was no need for table rapping, amnesia, automatisms etc., all this can go. Often the pair would simply sit at a table, wherever they were. Yeats would then frame questions and George would discourse upon the subject. She would not pretend to be in a trance or speak in a funny voice like 'Is there anybody there?'. This form of trance is one that we could all emulate - given enough practice. It is a more integrated approach, in which magick and one's ordinary life are less divided one from the other. Even the convention of using 'joined up' automatic script can be dispensed with given time. These things are *means to an end* not the end in itself. Once you understand the kind of awareness a trance is, you can often dispense with the trappings. This style of trancework or channeling is actually quite ancient and falls into a broad category of magick that is sometimes called the Apollonian style as opposed to the Dionysian system which is more energetic and exhausting.

Yeats asks in one of the trances, if any of his magical techniques, especially invocation, may be of use in analysis or for provoking the communicators. The answer is that he might use some variety of talismanic magick. The communicators' reply is thus:

'A symbol to be dipped in water after each night of sleep. Make a mantra over a small object give it to her to wear in sleep without saying what it is use(d) for. Charge with a simple clear image such as a flower.'

The purpose of this talisman is not necessarily to incubate a dream. It may indeed do that but it may also serve to facilitate the next day's trance dialogue. When asked what image to put on the talisman the communicators reply:

'Use a nature symbol not a planetary one.'

At this stage in his life Yeats was, as the communicators reminded him, using his own words 'nothing but the embittered sun' His over intellectual, solar nature needed a counterbalance. Along with this the communicators say that he should *not* use a 'planetary' sigil, of the kind that would have been familiar to him from his work in the Hermetic Order of the Golden Dawn. He should instead use a more natural image, such as a flower. This could be a stylized drawing of a flower, like a sigil or rapid intuitive representation of a flower. I think it could be an actual flower or even the essence of a flower such as perfume oil.

The communicators say:

'Put the moving image on the object and don't do it again or you will gradually lose the first simplicity of the thought.'

This is so like the sigilisation technique of Austin Spare, it is uncanny. I suggest it is a technique we could all try. I have done so now with success.

Exercise 2

Step One: Take a piece of clean cartridge paper.

Step two: Make the mind calm, and in an intuitive flash mark it with a natural symbol, perhaps a flower or even dropping some perfume oil on the talisman.

Step three: say a mantra over it. Interesting that the communicators use the term 'mantra', a Sanskrit term and not the most obvious one. But it accords well with the decidedly eastern flavour of the 'Yeatsian' magical system.

Step four: Sleep with it under your pillow.

Step five: neutralize the talisman by emersion in water the next day

This is what happened to me on one of the occasion I did this: I smelt some rose oil, which is one of the most magical of oils; note the occurrence of this in the name Rosicrucian etc etc. I had the following dream:

13th November 1995

In the dream I went to a country estate, called either Grift or perhaps Drift farm. It had a grand house with a memorial column up high on one of the hills. On one of the tenant farms nearby, was a gorge with perhaps the disused entrance to a well shaft. The farmer had permission to excavate this shaft. There was some connection between this and a mutilated carving in a nearby church. The Jacobean carvings had been beheaded, and although the heads had been retrieved from various dealers, it had never been restored. There was something sinister about the family whose tomb it was. As we took away the rough course of blocks that hid the entrance to the well shaft, we found a much more elaborate tomb inside. There were artifacts scattered everywhere, including a fine blue ancient Egyptian perfume vial, the lid still intact. There was danger that our efforts would be too crude and that we would loose as much as we could salvage. Before I could stop them, someone rinsed the perfume bowl in water, leaving only a tiny trace of the original contents for analysis. I saw the name Francis Barrett, perhaps his hidden tomb. [The place of FB's burial is currently unknown although there have been reports of a tomb in Kensal Green cemetery.] I knew we would need more equipment now for properly documenting what we were finding. A dog appeared and was much attracted by the aroma coming from inside the still sealed tomb. And a local labourer was also drawn to the place.

Sacred Marriage

Which stems from the communications. The transcripts show that it was a genuine collaboration, not merely Yeats, although his wife George, received very little credit and she wanted none either. (See Mills Harper p.19)

The published accounts say that what is missed out, is probably more significant than what is left in. 'I have *not* dealt with the whole of my subject, perhaps not even with the most important, writing nothing on the beatific vision, little of sexual love.'

What we might call the tantrik element in the ritual is omitted although by what little is said, it is clear that Yeats would have had a lot to say about the nature of sacred sexuality, his whole life was after all constructed between the three women who ruled his life. Furthermore, the initiation he got in this the second half of his life, came via his marriage, more especially the physical sexual relationship he had with his wife that opened certain doors. He hadn't been a virgin before this, but sexuality had obviously been a troubled area for him. Now the conflict was finally resolved and the marriage bed became a place of initiation.

This earthy feature of Yeats's life cannot be avoided. Even in supposedly puritanical Ireland, the issue is not dodged. In the Tower house I mentioned earlier, which is now a museum, you can see the Yeatses' bedroom, complete with some of the original furniture. Pride of place is given to a beautiful hand made pine bed that was according to the museum's display, the focus of many central spiritual events in the couple's life. On display near the bed is one of Yeats's 'tantrik' poems. It is called the 'Gift of Harun Al Rashid'.

Harun Al Rashid was the caliph of Baghdad in the 10th century. He was an exact contemporary of Charlemagne. This Christian despot converted people at the point of a sword. Harun Al Rashid figures in many stories of the Arabian Nights. He is the caliph who takes a new wife each night and has them put to death each morning. Until he meets Sheherazade, who tells him such a fascinating story that he keeps her alive until she has the opportunity to finish it.

The narrator of Yeats's poem is Kusta Ben Luka, a magical creation of Yeats's imagination. Kusta is something like an ancient Sufi master and dervish, who had been forcibly converted to the Byzantine faith, i.e. Christianity. Kusta is like many another magicians living in the modern age. Kusta is an ageing philosopher, perhaps diplomat and soldier, who like Yeats, had found love in the autumn of his life. The marriage was arranged, or is in some way artificial, but he discovered that his bride had actually been secretly wooing and following him for many years. She breathes new life into him and wakes him up. Kusta asks the question 'But what if I have lit upon a woman who so shares my thirst for those old crabbed mysteries, so strains to look beyond our life, an eye that never knew that strain would scarce seem bright and yet herself can seem youth's very fountain, being all brimmed with Life?'

Another character in the magical poem asks him to explain how all this came about. Kusta replies 'Upon a moonless night I sat where I could watch her sleeping form, And wrote by candle-light; but her form moved, and fearing that my light disturbed her sleep

I rose that I might screen it with a cloth. I heard her voice [say], 'Turn that I may expound /what's bowed your shoulder and made pale your cheek './ And [I] saw her sitting upright on the bed; /or was it she that spoke or some great Djinn? /I say that a Djinn spoke. A livelong hour; /.../Truths without *father* [my emphasis] came, truths that no book /Of all the uncounted books that I have read, /Nor thought out of her mind or mine begot, /Self born, high born and solitary truths,/ Those terrible implacable straight lines /Draw through the wandering vegetative dream,/ Even those truths that when my bones are dust /Must drive the Arabian host.'

In a manner strangely parallel to Crowley's earlier experience with his first wife Rose Kelly, something had spontaneously inspired both women to become spirit mediums.

'maybe twice in every month murmured the wisdom of the desert Djinns.'

'She keeps that ignorance, nor has she now / That first unnatural interest in my books.'

'The signs and shapes / All those abstractions that you fancied were / From the great Treatise of Parmenides; / All, all those gyres and cubes and midnight things / Are but a new expression of her body / Drunk with the bitter sweetness of her youth. / And now my utmost mystery is out. / A woman's beauty is a storm-tossed banner; / Under it wisdom stands, and I alone - / Of all Arabia's lovers I alone - / Nor dazzled by the embroidery, / nor lost In the confusion of its night-dark folds, / Can hear the armed man speak'.

The communications prompt Yeats to construct an imaginary persona. This had been a feature of Yeats's earlier life and indeed of many of the people around them. It was a doctrine of the Golden Dawn, at least this is one way of interpreting the adoption of magical names and mottoes, as magical altar egos. Yeats cultivated two personalities within himself, his motto in the Golden Dawn was Demon Est Deus Inversus - The Devil is the God Reversed, which alludes to this dualism. He often used twin characters in his personality, two of which he revived in *A Vision*, i.e. Michael Robartes and Owen Ahern. This is fully amplified in his new magical philosophy where there are perceived to be two forces in nature, but now they are male and female, solar and lunar.

The Gyres

The doctrine of the Gyres, Vortexes or spirals is the fullest reflection of his philosophy. The Hermetic dictum is said to be 'As Above, So Below, or as it is written in Ayurveda, a doctrine related to Tantrism: 'Man is the universe in miniature'. In all areas of life, in our personality, in history, in politics etc, there is a spirit at work, what Hegel might have called the spirit of an age. It is one of the axioms of Hermeticism that the world is a collection of thoughts in the mind of the cosmic spirit. Yeats compared this to a spiralling vortex. Thus at the beginning of the present astrological age, about 50BC when the age of Pisces began, there were two forces at work, one was a disintegrating force, the other a small but potent force of integration. This is like a seed of light within the period of maximum darkness, or a seed of chaos within the point of maximum light. This is an extension of the Taoist image of yin and yang. Thus, for example, 2000 years ago the Roman Empire having reached, using the poetic image the widest point of the gyre or vortex, was on the point of collapse. Within were the forces that come together in the new religions such as Christianity, which will reach their finest development a thousand years later in the Middle Ages. At the time Yeats wrote, these forces were overextended and at their point of collapse. The cycle was about to start again and a new tiny seed about to be recognized. Yeats prophesied this twin point of despair, chaos and seed of creativity in his poem 'The Second Coming'.

The same models are reflected not just in history but also in human personality. The model given to Yeats by the spirit communicators is therefore an integrated theory of personality and society. This is the perspective of modernism.

The Phases of the Moon

Finally then, I just want to look at one important example of the magical symbolism that stems from the channelled communication we have been discussing. When I first read this, I was immediately struck by the fact that in all the new tarots currently under construction, no one in my knowledge, has imposed a thoroughly lunar symbolism on the deck. The Yeatses' spirit guides suggested that this should be done. This runs quite counter to Yeats's earlier training in the Hermetic Order of the Golden Dawn. I would remind you that the basis of the modern tarot was more or less cooked up by the Golden Dawn. This includes the twenty-two major arcana, the cabalistic correspondences between them, the zodiac, the planets and the alchemical elements. This system, with some refinements has been more or less followed ever since. It is certainly the system taught to Yeats when he joined the Golden Dawn. More surprising then that, the spirit guides suggested a complete overthrow of this and the substitution of a twenty eight symbol system, aligned with the phases of the moon.

As an example, we can apply this twenty-eight category system to say the development of the human persona.

1. The void
2. Beginning of energy
3. Beginning of ambition
4. Desire for primary objects
5. Separation from innocence
6. Artificial individuality
7. Assertion of individuality
8. War between individuality and race
9. Belief takes place of individuality
10. The image breakers
11. The consumer, the pyre builders
12. The Fore runners
13. The sensuous man
14 The obsessed man
15 No description
16. The positive man
17 The daimonic man

18 The emotional man

19 The assertive man

20 The concrete man

21 The acquisitive man

22 Balance between ambition and contemplation

23 The receptive man

24 The end of ambition

25 The conditioned man

26 The multiple man also called the hunchback

27 The saint

28 The fool

Here's the corresponding passage from *A Vision*:

Phase Twenty-eight

Will - *The Fool*

Mask *(from phase 14)*. True - *Oblivion*. False - *Malignity*

Creative Mind *(from phase 2)*. True - *Physical activity*.

False - *Cunning*.

Body of Fate *(from Phase 16)* - *The Fool is his own* Body of Fate.

> *The natural man, the Fool desiring his Mask, grows malignant, not as the Hunchback, who is jealous of those that can still feel, but through terror and out of jealousy of all that can act with intelligence and effect.*

The whole twenty-eight are arranged in a figure called the great wheel, supposedly taken from a text called the *Speculum Angelorum et Hominum*, written by Giraldus,[7] although Yeats was the model for the portrait in the book.

The twenty-eight concepts, are divided into two halves, as in Tantrik/Hindu esoteric lore. Numbers 1 to 14 are ruled by the period from the new moon to the full moon, the bright fortnight in Hindu astrology. Phases 15 to 28 are ruled by the period of the waning moon, or dark fortnight in Hindu astrology.

The cycle is further divided by the quarter moons, thus the first quarter is Libra, ruled by Earth, second quarter by Cancer, ruled by Water, third quarter by Aries and Air, fourth quarter by Capricorn and Fire. This sequence reflects the Hindu progression of the elements rather than the more familiar astrological triplicities viz: Libra (Air); Cancer (Water); Aries (Fire) and Capricorn (Earth).

This is a very simplified schema of the Yeatsian 'tarot', which he takes almost a whole book to describe. But it is hopefully enough to show the quality of the magical work done by the Yeatses and that this has enduring value. With the current interest in tantrism, many of the ideas in the magical record make more sense, especially this twenty-eight 'day' cycle, which can be compared with the system of 'kalas' in tantrism, whereby, there is said to be a correspondence between the subtle energies in the body, and the phases of the moon. In the Yeatsian system, unlike the tantrik one, these changes seem to effect men as well as women. In fact he habitually uses the generic 'he' throughout the text. Thus the second quarter, from the half full to the full moon is connected with the heart, the period from the full to the half empty moon, the head, and the period from the half empty to the new moon the genitals. Which is another fascinating parallel with the tantrik triplicity of head, heart and genitals, as three primary chakras.

Well that's probably enough for now. The contents of the Yeatses's magical work, definitely would reward further study. We can see that Yeats, through the medium of his wife, was initiated into a new magical current that prompted him to restore the lost feminine and lunar side of his own personality, and suggest this as a project for all magicians. They seem to have discovered or rediscovered, by the use of sexual magick a genuine tantrik magical philosophy that was communicated to them in a most unusual way. I hope you agree.[8]

Appendix 1: The Phases of the Moon
Notes on compiling the chart

An experimental observational record of the phases of the moon and their magical and psychological impact. It should be used as an optional part of your diary. (copies available on request from mandrake@mandrake.uk.net.

It is part of an ongoing project of mine connecting lunar astrology with the Typhonian or Sethian magical tradition, and also the system of kalas from Hindu tantrism. You can if you wish give me feedback on the table from time to time.

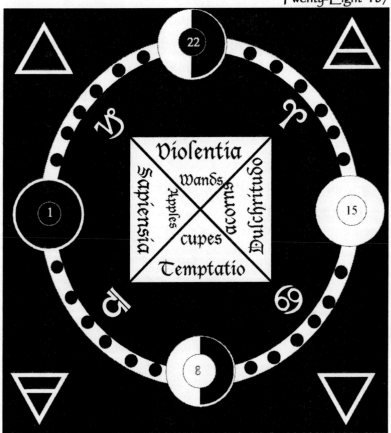

The Columns

1. *Solar Date* - the normal calendar date

2. *Occult Phase or Tarot* - these are symbolic and cosmological interpretations of the phases of the moon, adapted from the work of W B and George Yeats. The cycle can apply to the individual development over a single or many lifetimes.

3. *Accidental keyword* - If you have any interesting visions or dreams on that day, try to reduce its essence to a single key word and write that here.

4. *Days of lunar month*, starting with first day of new moon. The twenty-eight days are traditionally divided into four sections for each quarter. The period from the new to the full moon is known as the bright fortnight, that from the full moon to the dark of the moon as the dark fortnight.

5. *Personal code* - place a symbol here of an significant personal events that occur or recur during the month. For example, if you are a woman and you have your period, you could insert a dark circle here for each of the days.

The Rows

1. Twenty-eight day lunar clock/mandala a synthesis of Lokanath's sidereal model (See 'The Sri Yantra and Sidereal Astrology') and the 'Yeatsian' tarot, with some extra material from the ancient Egyptian stellar tradition. The moon-phases or kalas, reflect the essence of the seven traditional planets into the psyche, as represented by the inner triangle. These attributions are provisional. Built as a solid mandala it could have coloured pegs to show the current phase of the moon. Mandala could be used in place of usual pentacle as meditational devise (yantra). If you map the passage of the moon against a fixed point in the sky, it would actually take 27 days, 6 hours to return to that point. However, the distance from new moon to new moon is approximately 29 days. This is because a new moon, is, in astrological terms, a conjunction with the sun, and by the time the moon reaches the point in the sky it occupied 27 days earlier, the sun has also moved on in its orbit, and the moon has to travel for a further two days to make the conjunction. The extra (epagomenal) days on the month, can be accommodated by using the triangle with its three 'inner' planets. You may remember from elementary physics, that the ebb and flow of the tides, is determined by the conjunction and opposition (full moon) of the sun and moon. I.e as fluid bodies are sensitive to the wanderings of these 'planets' (in particular). Human beings (male and female) are mainly composed of water, so we could conclude that there is something akin to the tides at work in our own bodies and psyche.

2. Phase one is the new moon, also corresponding with geomantic north.

3. The zodiac signs mark the point of the solstice and equinoxes. These points also represent - loins, head, heart and organs of excretions respectively.

Phases of the Moon			Sheet Number: .2004.....	
Solar Day	Occult Phase or Tarot provisional	Accidental keyword	Lunar phase	Personal code
28th Jul	The Void		1	
29th Jul	Beginning of Energy		2	
	Beginning of ambition		3	
	Desire for primary objects		4	
	Separation from innocence		5	
	Artificial individuality		6	
	Assertion of individuality		7	

192 Tankhem

Phases of the Moon			Sheet Number: .2004.....	
Solar Day	Occult Phase or Tarot provisional	Accidental keyword	Lunar phase	Personal code
	War between individual and the collective		8	
	Belief takes place of individuality		9	
	The image breakers		10	
	The consumer - the pyre builders		11	
	The fore runners		12	
	The sensuous		13	
	The obsessed		14	

Phases of the Moon			Sheet Number: .2004.....	
Solar Day	Occult Phase or Tarot provisional	Accidental keyword	Lunar phase	Personal code
	The void of your own making		15	
	The positive person		16	
	The daimonic person		17	
	The emotional person		18	
	The assertive person		19	
	The concrete person		20	
	The acquisitive person		21	

Phases of the Moon			Sheet Number: .2004.....	
Solar Day	Occult Phase or Tarot provisional	Accidental keyword	Lunar phase	Personal code
	Balance between ambition and contemplation		22	
	The receptive person		23	
	The end of ambition		24	
	The conditioned person		25	
	The multiple person also called the Hunchback		26	
	The saint		28	
	The fool		28	

Invocation of the Moon

Ancient Greek vases show an ancient ritual known as drawing down the moon. Ovid's depiction of Medea in the *Metamorphoses* contains a lovely thaumaturgical prayer to Hekate that contains the lines:

'I draw down the bright blue moon from the sky
though brazen cymbals crash and thunder to keep her in her place;
even the chariot of the sun, my grandfather, grows pale at my song,
and I drain the color from the dawn for my potions.

Invocation of Hekate

(from Ovid's *Metamorphoses*)

O night, most faithful guardian of my secrets,
and golden stars who, moon-wed, succeed the brightness of the day;
You, Hekate, three-formed goddess, who knows my achievements and ordeals
and comes to aid my spells and works of magick art;
And you, O earth, you garden of herbs potent for the wise in sorcery;
you also, breezes and winds, mountains, rivers and lakes;
all spirits of the groves and of the night, come forth!

With your aid I can turn rivers to run backwards to their source
between their astonished banks;
I can soothe the stormy seas,
or rouse their placid surface with my songs;
The clouds will flee or thicken at my whim;
The winds will howl or disappear;
My spells and incantations could burn a dragon with its own fire

or harness it for me to ride.
The living rocks and trees would march if I willed it,
the oaks would uproot themselves, even whole forests;
At my bidding the mountains tremble,
the earth is twisted by dull rumblings,
and the ghosts arise from their tombs.

I draw down the bright blue moon from the sky,
though brazen cymbals crash and thunder to keep her in her place.
Even the chariot of the Sun, my grandfather, grows pale at my
song,
and I drain the colour from the Dawn for my potions.

Lo! I am Medea, the sorceress, your adorer, great Hekati!
It was you who dulled for me the fiery breath of the bulls,
and harnessed to the crooked plough those necks which had never
drawn a load.
You turned the warriors of the dragon's teeth to fight among
themselves,
you lulled to sleep the guardian serpent,
you sent the Fleece across the waters in my care.

Now, patron, give me this:
the spells of immortality, to make a man or woman like thee,
to restore the blush of youth to a cheek covered in furrows,
to turn weak sinews to engines of bronze,
to stoke the fiery breath of youth in withered lungs!
This you will do!
Not for nothing have the stars flashed in answer to my call!
Not for nothing have you sent your chariot,
drawn by a dragon-team!

Notes

1   Richard Ellmann, *Yeats, The Man and the Masks* (Penguin 1987) p. 223

2   Ellmann, p220.

3   p xiv

4   George Mills Harper, *The making of Yeats, A Vision* (Macmillan 1987) 2 vols introduction

5   For an interesting example see (R v Duncan [1944] KB 713 2 2 All ER 220) The last prosecution under the Witchcraft Act of 1735, repealed by the Fraudulent Mediums Act 1951. See *Stones Justice Manual* Volume 1, p1836, 1987

6   Ellmann p. 1

7   obvious pun on gyre.

8   Kalogera, Lucy Shepard, 1945- Yeats's Celtic mysteries / 1981 1977 Book, Thesis (Ph. D.)—Florida State University, 1977.

6 North

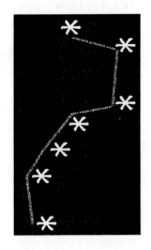

Most of us are familiar with the Crowley cultus. For those not so, I'd point out that in Crowley's grimoire *Magick - Liber ABA*, much of the really important instructional material is contained in appendices to the main text. Appendix II in *Magick* is entitled 'One Star In Sight' and is 'a glimpse of the structure and system of the great white brotherhood A∴A∴ A∴A∴ is often fleshed out as Argenteum Astrum, or Order of the Silver Star. This term A∴A∴ occurs as the name of an order in ancient Greece and there are conflicting opinions on the exact meaning of the term. This text sets out the magical work appropriate to the eleven grades of the A∴A∴ as envisioned by Crowley. I don't really intend to go into that here, if interested you can read the appendix for yourself. What interests me, as indeed it has interested others such as Kenneth Grant, is connecting this idea of 'one star in sight' with an actual constellation.

What led me to this material was a long time interest in the mythology and magick of the Egyptian deity Seth, who is supposedly the dark or opposing force in this ancient holy family of Isis, Osiris, Horus (or Anubis), Nepthys and Seth. All were born from Nuit who with her consort Geb and their father Amon completes the pantheon. Incidentally this eightfold pantheon is represented in the Temple of Seti I at Abydos as the seven shrines, connected by the eighth which is the overarching Nuit: 'above Nuit, the mother of us all unfolds'

I don't really expect you to accept the existence of these deities. I think we use these terms as some sort of symbolic language for discussion of what is in the psyche. As is well known, ancient Egyptian religion was very stellar, i.e. they liked to make correspondences between things they could see in the night sky and the kinds of god forms that moved around in their heads. Each of the eight important gods had a stellar equivalent. The two most important constellations were the Great Bear (known also as 'the Imperishable Stars') and Orion. Both were regarded as deities. The Dog-star Sirius or Sothis was chief of all stars because it was the herald of the inundation and its reappearance before dawn at the summer solstice was celebrated as a religious festival. It was dedicated to Isis and there is a legend that the tears she shed at the annual death of Osiris caused the inundations.'(Murray TSTWE p. 189)

It is widely believed by some of the magi, that there is some link between Sothis/Sirius and Seth. In the Osiris cult, Osiris was drowned by Seth - a possible parallel with the way in which the vegetation of Ancient Egypt was overwhelmed and 'killed' by the annual flood, at the same time refreshing the land and making way for new growth. It seems an obvious step to make the star Sirius that signals the beginning of the flood, some kind of personification of Seth, the storm deity who ultimately causes the flood. There are however problems with this idea - during the time of the popularity of the Osiris cult, direct rain and its personification Seth, was not necessary for the ecosystem and neither was it welcome. The flooding of the Nile and the use of irrigation refreshed the ecosystem. In fact the ancient Egyptians made a correspondence between Seth and the Constellation *Ursa Major*. The ancient Egyptians knew this constellation under the name Meskhetyu, the Bull, although in later times its name changed to the Great Bear. Both totemic beasts occur in later Invocations with veiled Setian undercurrents. Although Ursa Major is always visible in the night sky, it does in the course of twenty-four hours, 'dance' around the pole star and as well as rotate on its own axis.[1] This outer lip of the 'gourd' always points to the Pole Star, currently Polaris (just to confuse matters Polaris in found in the constellation *Ursa Minor* - although four thousand years ago the Pole-star was located in the constellation Draco).

To the ancient Egyptians, the constellation we call *Ursa Major was* Seth. It is as well to remember that in the cycle of the year, Osiris is not the only sacrificial victim - whilst at the summer solstice Osiris is sacrificed by water, at the winter solstice Seth was sacrificed by fire, so the two great constellation/dragons, revolve and replace each other over and over again?

Whether I've got this cycle quite right - the fact is that elements of this mythos have traveled quite widely, and are found in many other parallel mythologies. The clearest connecting link is the appearance of the constellation Ursa Major in several outwardly diverse magical systems - its is a secret link if you like - here are some examples:

The Setian connection with the cult of Mithras as revived, (not created in the Greek and Roman world) is seen in *Mithras liturgie* (H D Betz -The Greek Magical Papyri In Translation - PGM IV line 700) This is an ancient magical 'grimoire' dated from several centuries before the birth of Christ.

> 'Now when they take their place, here and there, in order, look in the air and you will see lightning bolts going down, and lights flashing, and the earth shaking, and a god descending, a god immensely great, having a bright appearance, youthful, golden-haired, with a white tunic and a golden crown and trousers, and holding in his right hand a golden/ shoulder of a young bull: this is the Bear which moves and turns heaven around, moving upward and downward in accordance with the hour.'

In this cult the central mystery revolved around the sacrifice by Mithras (a god with qualities very like the Egyptian Horus) of the Bull, (although as in ancient Egypt, this bull was not a full grown adult, but a young and more manageable bull calf, of which the foreleg, which resembles the constellation Ursa Major, was offered.

Another example comes from the Leyden Papyrus:

'(1) And you set up your [planisphere?] and you stamp on
the ground with your foot seven times and recite these
charms to the Foreleg, turning {?) to the North seven
times (2) and you return down and go to a dark recess.'

This is the beginning of a 'spell' for divination by use of a lamp.
The constellation is the easiest way to fix the northern point for any
ritual work.

Yet another example comes from the Book of Job (ix.9), often
regarded by the magi as giving an insight into the real nature of the
dark initiator Shaitan, who tests Job's faith in Jahweh.

Job says:...
But how can a man be just before God?
If one wished to contend with him,
One could not answer him once in a thousand times.
He is wise in heart and mighty in strength
- who has hardened himself against him and succeeded? -
He who removes mountains and they know it not...
Who alone stretched out the heavens and trampled the waves
Of the sea;
Who made the Bear and Orion,
The Pleiades and the chambers of the south.

These last few lines mark out the four directions of space using
stellar coordinates. And finally here's another important example,
this time from Taoism,

'To dance the eight trigrams requires some tricky technical information. As maybe you'll want to do a ritual along these lines one day, I'll give a brief synopsis of the principle of the ceremony and hope that this is not too complicated a task. Plenty of Taoist rites make use of the dance of Yü. First the eight signs are projected on the ground. Look at the illustrations now and you can see that the order of the dance is made up out of the appearance of numbers in a magical square. In the ordinary arrangement, the dance of Yü begins in the north and ends in the south. The dance pattern can be applied to the circle of early and later heaven, that is, the dance steps remain the same but the signs visualized in each direction differ. When you use the circle of early heaven you begin with the receptive and end with the creative, using the circle of later heaven the dance begins with dark water and ends with bright fire. So far this is a fairly simple matter. Some found it too simple and introduced complications. There are several schools of thunder magic that were developed to counter and combat the malevolent sorceries of the Tao of the left with its violent spirits. In the performance of thunder magic the dance of Yü is a key element. Not the simple version of the dance but a variety that was invented around the fifth century to introduce a bit of exclusive secret knowledge and confusion. In the circle of the eight signs, Ken, The Mountain represents not only a cloud covered peak but also (look at the shape of the sign) the entrance of a cave. In this aspect, the sign receives the title "The Gate of Life" and becomes a crucial focus of power. In the usual arrangement of the chart of the later heaven, the sign Ken is in the northeast. The thunder magicians, however, decided that the position of the gate is not fixed but changes every few hours. In their system the gate of the otherworld has to be found. The position of this gate depends on the constellation known as the Great Bear (Ursa Major), also called the Big Dipper or the Great Wagon. If you look at it as a wagon, you can see that the shaft points in a certain direction. As the wagon moves around the polar star, the direction of the shaft keeps changing. If the shaft points at the east, for instance, the gate to the otherworld is also in the east. This means that the eastern trigram functions as the gate. As the wagon keeps moving, there is a new gate every couple of hours. It is part of the complications in ritual thunder magic Taoism to calculate the direction of the gate. In practice, the gate shifts from trigram to trigram as the Great Bear moves around the centre of heaven. The gate represents the weakest and most dangerous point in the circle, as it seems strong on the outside but is weak further in. You might argue that the sign Kun, the receptive, is a lot weaker than Ken. Though this is true, a Chinese strategist would not dream of attacking at a spot where an attack is expected. Weak as Kun is, it might conceal an ambush. Ken, looking strong but being weak, is a much better choice. At this sign, the otherworld is closest. The dangerous Chia spirits use it to come to earth, so do various disease spirits, and generally, people fear to lose their vital Ch´i energy through this gate. The deceased leave earth through this doorway, but they also use this gate to escape from hell and to ascend to heaven. It is also the point where the thunder magic Taoist begins and ends the dance of Yü, and from which the power of the thunder-breath is summoned. Sealing this dangerous place is among the first priorities of the practising ritualist.'

(Jan Fries, *Living Midnight - three movements of the Tao*)

I could go on but maybe you've got the picture. Almost any text, which mentions this constellation the Great Bear, will have an interesting magical undercurrent and very often will yield a lost and obscure element of the ancient magick of the Setians, from which the magi descend. It is for this reason that I suggest we always honour this constellation and use it as much as possible as a connection in our magick.

Appendix: The Great Bear rite

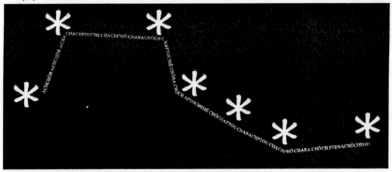

Opening Rite
Seven are the sacred sounds of the void

A   E   Ê   I   O   Y   Ô,

I call upon you, the greatest power in heaven,
in the name of the bear.
You appointed by the lord god to turn with a strong hand
the holy pole'

NIKAROPLÊX. [Polaris in the lesser Bear]

'Listen to me, Amon Ra, hear the holy [prayer].
You who hold together the universe and bring to life the whole
world.'

THÔZOPITHÊ
EUCHANDAMA
ÔCHRIENTHÊR
OMNYÔDÊS
CHÊMIOCHYNGÊS
IEÔY
(perform a sacrifice)

THERMOUTHER
PSIPHIRIX PHROSALI
KANDTHIMEÔ ZAZZEMIA
ÔPER PEROMENÊS
RÔTHIEU ÊNINDEU
KORKOUNTHO EUMEN MENI
KÊDEUEA KÊPSEOI
(add the usual)

THÔ ZO PTAH,
'Bear, greatest goddess ruling heaven, reigning over the pole of the stars, highest, beautiful-shining goddess, incorruptible element, composite of the all, all-illuminating, bond of the universe.'

Have the following square:

A	E	Ê	I	O	Y	Ô,
E	Ê	I	O	Y	Ô	A
Ê	I	O	Y	Ô	A	E
I	O	Y	Ô	A	E	Ê
O	Y	Ô	A	E	Ê	I
Y	Ô	A	E	Ê	I	O
Ô	A	E	Ê	I	O	Y

'You who stand on the pole,
you whom the lord god appointed to turn the holy pole with a
strong hand':
THÔZOPITHÊ (formula)

Petition to the sun at sunset:

Formula
'THÊNÔR,
O Atum,
SAN THÊNÔR,
'I beseech you, Lord, may the play and the lord of the Bear
devote themselves to me'
(while petitioning sacrifice armara. Do it at sunset.)

Offering for the procedure:

4 drams of frankincense, 4 drams of myrrh, 2 ounces each of cassia
leaf and/ of white pepper, 1 dram of bdellion, 1 dram of asphodel
seed, 2 drams each of amomon, of saffron, of terebinth storax, 1
dram of wormwood — of vetch plant, priestly Egyptian incense,
the complete brain of a black ram/ Combine these with white
Mendesian wine and honey, and make pellets of bread.

Phylactery for the procedure:
Wear a wolf's knucklebone, mix juice of vetch and of pondweed
in a censer. Write in the middle of the censer this name:

'THERMOUTH* EREPSIPHIRIPHI PISALI (24 letters),
and in this way make an offering.

* *Thermutis or Egyptian Rennutet, Egyptian harvest goddess and Fate*
Based on PGM IV,1275 -1322

The hundred lettered name of Typhon
Curved as a star and bind it in the middle of the core with the letters
showing

ACHCHÔR ACHCHÔR

ACHACHACHPTOUMI

CHACHCHÔ CHARACHÔCH

CHAPTOUMÊ CHÔRA CHÔCH

APTOUMIMÊ CHÔCHAPTOU

CHARACHPTOU CHACHCHÔ

CHARA CHÔCH PTENACHÔCHEOU

Result

In the desert I burn your incense, placing my candles in the shape of the constellation. Across time the greatest of all your ancient priests appears to me, his face an embalmer's miracle - Sethos. I am your servant, teach me the ancient ways of he/she who upholds Polaris. It is good, I hear you say.

It was, fate that led me to Abydos, this unpromising place in the desert. Abydos, such a place, the most sacred on earth. The very name is a word of power. It was, and perhaps always was, a place sacred to Osiris/Orion - give him his due. Although the most ancient sacred enclosure of that god, is not where I planned to build my temple. The first temenos of Osiris is a good mile away across the desert. But in my day this was an old place and becoming very overcrowded. There was, you see, a need for a new sacred enclosure to the god and this task fell to me, the scion of a new dynasty. Throughout my life I worked to undo the harm done by the worshippers of the one god - Aten - I shall not name them, you know who they are. As a Setian, I am tolerant of all the gods, although for one in particular, I have a greater love, that is natural.

But the disasters that befell us when we turned from the old polytheistic ways are surely the real reason why I hate Akenaten and his family so much. If it had worked for us, then so be it, even the wanton acts of vandalism on the shrines of the 'god of existence' Amon, could be tolerated, if nature had not rebelled against us. Even now I doubt if I shall be able to undo the damage wrought by them, and they say I am a fearsome General. I doubt if even my warrior sons will be able to restore order and stop the tide of Assyria and their treacherous Hebrew cohorts. They are building an empire, or so they think, and when you have land on your mind, honour goes out the window. But history has a bitter lesson in store for them, if they think they can play footsy with the Assyrian and not end up with spike through their heels! But I digress.

I am a man of Seth, as are all my family. Born to holy orders in his service. And yet I was pharaoh.

Some say you were the greatest pharaoh that has lived.' I interject.

'Thankyou - I have heard this said also.'

Appendix II: The Hexagram

A useful ritual in this tradition.

The Lesser Ritual of the Hexagram

This ritual is to be performed after the 'Lesser Ritual of the Pentagram'

I.   Stand upright, feet together. left arm at side, right across body, holding Wand or other weapon upright in the median line. Then face East and say.

II.   I N R I
        Yod Nun Resh Yod
        Virgo, Isis, Mighty Mother
        Scorpio Apophis Destroyer
        Sol, Osiris, Slain and Risen
        Isis, Apophis, Osiris, IAO

III   Extend the arms in the form of a cross and say
        'The sign of Osiris Slain.'

IV.   Make the appropriate sign and say
        'The sign of the Mourning of Isis'

V.   Raise the arms to sixty degrees and say
        'The sign of Apophis and Typhon

VI.   Cross the arms on the breast, bow the head and say:
        'The sign of Osiris risen'

VII.   Extend the arms again as in III and cross them again as in VI saying:
        'L U X, Lux, The light of the Cross.

VIII.   With the magical weapon trace the Hexagram of Fire in the East saying:

ARARITA- 'One is his beginning; One is His Individuality; His Permutation is One'

(This hexagram consists of two equilateral triangles, both apices pointing upwards. Begin at the top of the upper triangle and trace it in a clockwise direction. The top of the lower triangle should coincide with a central point of the upper triangle. To invoke the double/tankhem current do not use a single point but both hands (one for each triangle) at the same time, each trigramme may equal the three worlds)

IX.   Trace the Hexagram of Earth in the South, saying: 'ARARITA etc'
(This hexagram has the apex of the lower triangle pointing downwards, and it should be capable of inscription in a circle.

X.   Trace the Hexagram of Air in the West, saying: 'ARARITA etc'
(This hexagram is like that of Earth; but the bases of the triangles coincide, forming a diamond.)

XI.   Trace the hexagram of Water in the North, saying: 'ARARITA etc'
(This hexagram has the lower triangle placed ubove the upper, so that their apices coincide.

XII.   Repeat I-VII

The Banishing Ritual is identical, save that the direction of Hexagrams must be reversed.

7 The crooked wand

'The Wand is the principal weapon of the Magus, and the *name* of that wand is the Magical Oath.' Thus writes Crowley in one of the highly informative chapters on ceremonial contained in his masterwork *Liber ABA*, otherwise known as *Magick*. 'The Magical Will,' he continues, 'is the wand in your hand by which the Great Work is accomplished, by which the Daughter is not merely set upon the throne of the Mother, but assumed into the Highest.'

In the Thoth Tarot the 'Prince of Wands' in various versions drawn by Frieda Harris is shown holding the so-called Phoenix wand as wielded by the grade Adeptus Major in the Hermetic Order of the Golden Dawn. Several of these wands were modeled on the ceremonial sceptres of Ancient Egypt. But interestingly the so-called 'Phoenix-wand' is actually the 'Was' or 'sceptre of well being'. The iconographers of the Golden Dawn seemed to have missed the fact that the head of this scepter is actually that of Seth

Colossal *Was* Scepter from Ombos in Upper Egypt and exhibited in the Victoria & Albert Museun, London

and not the solar image they presumed. It might also be that the original wielders of the Was-scepter were also in denial about its original meaning. This fact is not, as far as I know, common knowledge amongst current Golden Dawn savants, which may account for the fact that some modern realizations of the wand have moved even further away from its original functionality and indeed power. In very ancient Egypt of Old Kingdom times and before, Egyptian men often carried a stick or staff of some kind. Sometimes these were like the European quarterstaff.[1] One suggestion I got from my friend the cunning man Jack Daw, is that the original of the Was sceptre may have been the kind of hooked

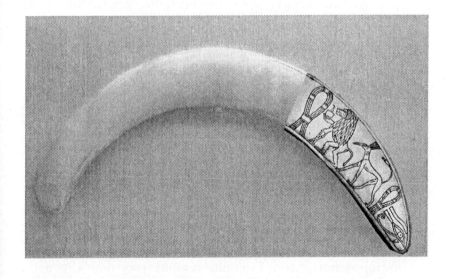

Exhibit labelled 'Magic Knife' from National Museum of Scotland, Edinburgh, (with detail superimposed). Hippopotamus ivory, Prob X11th dynasty c1890BC, Thebes(?). Length 13.5 ins. Engraved with figures and symbols designed to ward off evil beings and noxious creatures from the child's sleeping place.'

wand used to hold back grass or wheat for the stroke of a sickle. It serves to protect the harvester's left hand from being accidentally struck by the blade. If true this maybe explains the Was-sceptre's name as 'Sceptre of well being'. The significance of the forked foot of the Was-sceptre is a mystery, it may be connected with the binding of the sceptre to the arm or perhaps have a function to do with the warding off of snakes, a common enough hazard of harvesters, The Was-sceptres of Middle Kingdom times became purely mystical or symbolic. The image of the 'Was-scepter' also appeared in carved decorated borders on Egyptian reliefs, where two or more sceptres hold up the vault of heaven. The latter being yet another reference to the power of Seth whose iron pillars hold up the heavens that which he occasionally threatens to remove and use as a weapon. But still the Sceptre shows an unexpected connection between Seth and agriculture and this is worthy of some thought.

But there was another wand commonly used in ancient Egypt and this too bore an image of Seth, as indeed one would expect in operations of a more magical / esoteric nature. Many examples of this kind of wand have been found, and some of the finest are displayed in the more important museum collections. Most museums have numerous other examples of this type of wand in their vaults. This instrument is constructed from a male hippopotamus tusk. I would remind you that the male hippopotamus is viewed as a totem of Seth. The more aggressive male hippopotamus were a favorite quarry of the ancient Egyptian hunter. The tusk shape shows a clear Setian association, both from its material and decoration. Its curved nature reminds us of the lunar mysteries. We are told that the wands were used in acts of highly personal magick, the most quoted example being to ward off hungry demons during the critical moments of childbirth and infancy. This is the realm of popular magick as opposed to the more exoteric variety of magical religion practiced in the temples. I think it would probably be wrong to draw too impervious a line between both realms. And in fact the use of the hippopotamus tooth wand shows a clear connection between both realms through the agency of Seth, here equally at home among the holy family of the temples and scaring lesser demons in the hearth.

Examples of such wands show they were well used and treasured over several generations. The pointed tip shows signs of wear, as if it has been repeatedly used to draw mystical signs, in sand or clay. It is also likely that the wand was used to draw protective circles, like the 'cartouche' inscribed around the name of the King. When the tips broke off from repeated use, the ends were pinned back in place.

The ubiquitous nature of the head of Seth is something that warrants meditation. To acquire such a wand in the modern world might prove difficult. I suggest perhaps carved or shaped wood, coated with ivory coloured paint or perhaps resin. The more linear Was sceptre suggests the throwing outwards or the more static instantiation of magical power. The curved or hooked hippopotamus wand suggests several additional functions; the drawing of sigils mentioned above, as a sigil itself, laid beneath a bed or perhaps hung on a wall. But also I feel the drawing of things to the magician - in order to use, spear or bind them to ones power.

Notes

1   B William C Hayes, *The Scepter of Egypt: a background for the study of the Egyptian antiquities in the Metroplitan Museum of Art*, 2 Vols, Abrams, NY 1953

Appendix

Guardians of the Dragon

In August 1997, an idea arose to form a new magical group called the *Guardians of the Dragon*. For some time my spiritual focus has been the Oxford based magical group known as OGDOS. Oxford has always had a long connection with the dragon symbol. An important dragon myth is recorded in the *Mabinogi*. The foundation saint of Oxford (Frideswide) calls upon the assistance of 'dragon' Saint Margaret (see *Strange Oxford*). Some of my favourite magical techniques have a connection with dragon energy eg seething uses a core myth of a stella and an earth dragon. Many of the magical systems we know about work with various manifestations of dragon/serpent lore - eg Tantrism, Voodoo, etc.

Many years ago, I was initiated into a tantrik secret society and mystery school known as AMOOKOS. It also seems significant to me that the secret chiefs of this tantrik sect are called dragon lords. It seems reasonable to me that a major intention for any of our rituals would be the honouring and calling of these dragon lords.

The rituals people most relate to, are those connected with the eight festivals calendar (The calendar of two dragons). In my opinion this is a very old calendar with roots going back to ancient Mesopotamia and the cult of Inanna/Pro-serpina. In other words it has deep roots in our psyche. This calendar fits well with a fairly eclectic schema, ie working rituals from several different traditions. But it occurs that this mythos could have a closer coordination to the time of year. Here is my provisional dragon calendar:

Samhain	November 1st	(Symbolic death)*
Yule - feast	December 21st	Burning of Seth's tail/
Imbolc	January 31st	1st Judgement
Equinox	March 21st	2nd Judgement
Beltaine	May 2nd	Rite of Pan
Solstice	June 20/21st	Osiris Drowned by Seth
Lammas	August 1st	Tantrik/Ganesha ritual
Equinox	Sept 21st	Mithraic rite

There is no general agreement of the central myth of the year - in my schema is goes as so

Yule-	Birth	
Imbolc	-	Childhood and protection by the mother
Equinox	-	The Return

Beltain	-	Magical conflict
Solstice	-	Sacrifice
Lammas	-	Harvest
Equinox	-	Trial
Samhain	-	Quest for new life in the Underworld

This is an ancient dark dragon lord, sometimes called Seth. I have found it interesting to draw down this power from time to time. Seth seems to have made it into British mythology through the story of St George and the Dragon (See Griffith *The Conflict of Seth and Horus*). St George's day is April 23rd . (Seth also connects with Oxford through his animal form as Old English Long Horn cattle, a direct blood relative of the Texas Long Horn.).

Openings

Every ritual needs a good opening rite. Initially this might entail using a universal opening like the pentagram rite. Whether this is the final choice, the feeling seems to be, that this should be used at the beginning of all rituals, and that *all* those present should chant it together, so it becomes less of an individual rite and a more collective experience. Given the eclectic nature of the calendar it might be objected that the pentagram stems from a particular style of magick, and that this could be discordant to the core work of the session. In partial answer to this point, it could be argued that the pentagram is in fact, far broader than the Kabbalistic system from which we learn it. This is because Kabbalah is itself an eclectic tradition, a fusion of Gnostic, Hermetic and Egyptian magical concepts, that were thrown together in the civilization of ancient

Alexandria. However, as a possible corrective to this, it might be acceptable to use another popular banishing - from the Nath tantrik tradition. This is particularly appropriate because of the preponderance of dragon symbolism in the Nath current. Here is the rite:

(In the version I have there, are no gestures for invoking the quarters, nor are there any names of power for vibration. In line with my own theories about the links between Tantrism and Egyptian Magick (Tankhem); I suggest adding a section here derived from the Greek Magical Papyri. You may indeed notice a similarity between the Kabbalistic Cross and this insertion, this is, in my opinion no accident.) I like to start my banishing with the 'Abydos Arrangement', but if it is your will you could substitute your own tradition at this point.

Face North and try to see the constellation Ursa Major.
Draw down its power and say:
Guardians of the House of Life at Abydos
Before me In the East: Nepthys
Behind me in the West Isis
On my right hand in the South is Seth
And on my left hand, in the North Horus
For above me shines the body of Nuit
And below me extends the ground of Geb
And in the centre abideth the 'Great Hidden God'

Mnemonic:

FAther GEt GAme to FEEd the HOt NEw hOme.

1. Now turn to the East, form both hands into fists and raise them up and to the left of your head, now vibrate the first vowel long and hard - AAAAAAA -

2. Now turn to the North and stretching your right hand in front of your vibrate the second vowel EEEEEEE, using the mnemoic gEt as above.

3. Then turn to the West and extend both hands in front of you and vibrate ÊÊÊÊÊÊÊas in GAme

4. Then turn to the South and drawing both hands to your stomach vibrate IIIIIII as in fEEd

[Whether one remains facing South or returns to face the East depends upon the operation in hand]

5. Now bend over and reach out to the Earth vibrating OOOOOOO as in HOt

6. Then gradually unfolding, come up and place your hands on your heart and vibrate YYYYYYY as in NEw

7. Finally stretching up to the heavens vibrate Ô Ô Ô Ô Ô Ô Ô as in HÔme.

(Now make the sign of the (invoking) pentagramme in the air in front of you and vibrate

Ou, Eye, EE, Aa, Uh)

Turn to the North, bow and visualise the form of a naked young goddess with a peaceful smiling face, her skin is green and she sits on the back of a bull.

(Again make the sign of the (invoking) pentagram and vibrate Ou, Eye, EE, Aa, Uh)

Turn to the South, bow and visualise the form of naked young goddess with skin the colour of fire. With flaming eyes, who sits astride a lion.

(Again make the sign of the (invoking) pentagram and vibrate Ou, Eye, EE, Aa, Uh)

Turn to the West, bow and visualise the form of a naked young goddess, blue in colour, glistening with moisture, with large beautiful eyes, riding a goose or swan.

(Again make the sign of the (invoking) pentagram and vibrate Ou, Eye, EE, Aa, Uh)

Finally
Honour the Earth, bending over, touching the Earth say:
'O' as in 'rope'

and then the sky, having both hands on your head say:
'Ô' as in 'bow'.

Based on PGM X111 824-834

Index

Printed in the United Kingdom
by Lightning Source UK Ltd.
102687UKS00001B/331-339